For my brothers...
I'll always have your back...

Author: **Boulder**, M.M.
Title: THE HOUSE THAT JACK BUILT.
ISBN: 9798678061706
Target Audience: Adult

Subjects:
Psychological Thriller, Domestic Thriller, Serial Killer Thriller

This is a work of fiction, which means it's made up. Names,
characters, peoples, locales, and incidents (stuff that happens in the
story) are either gifts of the ether, products of the author's resplendent
imagination or are used fictitiously, and any resemblance to actual
persons, living or dead or dying, businesses or companies in operation
or defunct, events, or locales is entirely coincidental.

Read more by **M.M. Boulder**

Psychological Thrillers

MY BETTER HALF
THE HOUSE THAT JACK BUILT
MY ONE AND ONLY
(Coming Soon)

Writing as **M.M. Crumley**

THE LEGEND OF
ANDREW RUFUS

BOOK 1: DARK AWAKENING
BOOK 2: BONE DEEP
BOOK 3: BLOOD STAINED
BOOK 4: BURIAL GROUND
BOOK 5: DEATH SONG
BOOK 6: FUNERAL MARCH
BOOK 7: WARPATH

www.mmboulder.com

M.M. Boulder

THE HOUSE THAT
JACK BUILT

Never Give Up The Ghost

Pronunciation Guide:

Sian (Siân): Welsh, pronounced "Sharn"

Bronwen: Welsh, pronounced "BRAHN-wen"

Áine: pronounced ON-ya, is an Irish Goddess of summer, love, protection, fertility, wealth and sovereignty. Also known as the Goddess of Luck and Magick

Chapter One

"I totally smeared you!" twenty-four-year-old Sian Ellis crowed as she trotted up the stone walkway towards the side door.

"Just because you won doesn't mean you beat me," her older brother Gavin replied with a snort.

"That's exactly what it means, you numbskull," she laughed as she pushed the heavy, wooden door open. She stepped into the anteroom off the kitchen, then stumbled to a halt, tennis racket slipping from her suddenly numb fingers and tumbling to the floor with a clatter.

"What's wrong?" Gavin asked, pushing past her.

Sian didn't respond. She couldn't. There was blood everywhere. On the floor, on the walls, on the doorway. So much blood. Brilliantly red, pulsating with energy and death. Sian could feel it, and it made her nauseous.

The floor to ceiling mirrors on either side of the doorway had been broken, and the blood shimmered on the shards, reflecting red and silver all over the hallway.

"How could anyone lose so much blood?" she whispered, beginning to think Alice was playing a nasty prank or they had just walked into a game of solve the murder.

That's when she saw the headless man lying in the middle of the room. Her heart stuttered, and her stomach rolled. She could see the bones in his neck. She could see his air pipe. He wasn't a prank. He was real. And he was very, very dead.

She fought a wave of dizziness, leaning on the wall for support. The smell of freshly baked bread was mixing with the metallic scent of the blood, and it was all she could do to keep from vomiting.

"Who is that?" she whispered frantically, her eyes scanning the hallway for the man's head. "Who killed him, Gavin? Why is he here?"

Gavin didn't respond, just cursed under his breath, pulled the knife he'd carried since he turned sixteen, and walked slowly forward. Towards the bloody kitchen doorway.

Sian pinched herself, trying to wake up. This couldn't be real. If she looked hard enough she'd see the walls were really made of pudding and the blood was just cherry sauce and she'd wake up hungry.

But when she opened her eyes the blood was still blood, coating everything, and Gavin was almost to the body. Sian leaped forward and grabbed his arm.

"What're you doing?" she stuttered. "We have to call the police. That man's dead... I mean... He doesn't have a head!"

"No," Gavin replied, voice rough. "We need to sweep the house to see if they're still here. Stay right behind me."

She didn't have to ask him who "they" were. He meant their family. Mom and Dad, Grandma, Owen, and Alice. Surely they weren't here. Surely they were okay. But someone had killed that man. Sian shuddered. It couldn't have been one of her family.

But where were they? Why hadn't her dad called them and told them what had happened, that there was a dead man in the hallway? Why couldn't she hear Grandma's demanding voice telling someone to clean up this mess?

"Sian, now!" Gavin hissed.

She tried to step forward, but her feet wouldn't budge. They didn't want to go near the blood. They didn't want to go near the dead man. They didn't want to know what was in the kitchen.

Gavin grabbed her hand, and she looked at him. His blue eyes were deeper than she'd ever seen them. Deep and full of an emotion she was too scared to identify.

"Listen, Sian," he said softly. "I need you to be strong right now. I need you to be brave. We have to go into the kitchen. What if Mom's in there? What if she needs our help?"

That was the problem. What if Mom WAS in there? It was too quiet. Everything was too quiet. All Sian could hear was her own ragged breathing. Why hadn't Owen or Mom, anyone, called them?

"Sian!" Gavin snapped.

She stared at him. She'd never seen him like this. He was usually so carefree and laid-back, so goofy. But he wasn't goofy now. His face was stone, and his words were harsh. He knew what was in the kitchen. He knew.

"Okay," she mumbled, wishing she still believed she could do anything as long as Gavin was with her.

"Stay behind me," he ordered again and stepped forward towards the kitchen.

She took a small step forward, and something crunched under her foot. She glanced down. Her grandma's prized Van Briggle vase was broken beyond recognition, purple fragments mixing with the glass of the mirrors. It didn't make sense. Nothing was making sense.

"Sian!" Gavin hissed.

He was nearly to the kitchen now, and he was waiting impatiently for her. She started to move forward again, but the floor between them was coated in blood. She swallowed a gag. There was no way she could reach him without stepping in it.

She tried to take another step, but her foot hovered just above the blood.

"NOW!" Gavin snapped.

She closed her eyes and stepped down. Her shoe squished, and she shuddered, then stepped forward again and again, walking just on her tippy toes, moving steadily towards Gavin.

She gagged as she stepped carefully over the dead man's body, then stepped into the kitchen behind Gavin, swallowing a scream as everything came into view.

There was a bloody stub of a hand on the kitchen counter, butcher knife still buried deeply in the glossy wooden countertop. A man was sprawled across the breakfast table, telephone cord wrapped around his neck. Another man was face down in a pool of blood on the floor, several kitchen knives buried to their handles in his back.

Sian closed her eyes. Everything was so quiet. Quieter than their house had ever been. She couldn't keep going. If Dad were here he would have...

She shook her head, trying to erase the thought. They were probably just out back or at the store. They hadn't been here. They surely hadn't killed these men. Everything was okay. They would find everyone, and they would laugh about how scared she was.

"We have to call the police," she mumbled, shaking all over.

"Shut up!" Gavin hissed, stepping over a body on the floor and heading towards the doorway leading to the formal dining room.

She wanted to run outside and keep running. She wanted to scream. She wanted her mom. But she followed him slowly, trying to tamp down her fear and her horror.

This has to be a dream, Sian thought, stopping by the table and staring at the strangled man's purple face. She'd fallen asleep reading again, and this was a dream. She had to stop reading horror novels. They were probably rotting her brain.

"Sian!" Gavin snapped.

She started to look up from the dead man, but then she noticed he'd fallen into a bowl of cereal and milk had splattered everywhere. The milk was mixing with blood, creating strange little pink puddles on the floor. Who had been eating cereal? Whose blood was on the floor?

"Sian, I need you to stay with me!"

Gavin never demanded, never ordered. He always said things with a laugh. Why was he suddenly so serious? This was a dream. It wasn't real.

Sian walked to him in a daze. She'd wake up any minute now. She'd wake up, and she'd find Gavin. They'd laugh about her crazy dream and go play their tennis match. She would beat him, because she always did, and they would come home and eat a huge breakfast. Just like they always did.

They walked down the hallway, following the blood. The dining room was empty and bloodless, so Gavin passed it by and kept going until he stepped out into the main entryway.

She heard him gasp. She saw him run forward. She saw him pull their mother off the floor and into his arms. She saw all the blood. Saw the way their mother's head rolled limply to the side, and part of her knew she was dead. But it was just a dream.

Sian walked forward slowly, feeling like she was caught in some kind of frozen moment. Time had stopped, and she could barely move.

Gavin was crying, and she didn't know why. "Mom's not really dead," she whispered. "This is just a dream."

His face was colorless and his eyes full of grief when he looked at her. "Oh Sian," he groaned. "I..." He didn't go on, but something in his eyes changed, hardened, resolved. He kissed their mom's head, laid her gently on the floor, and stood, grabbing Sian's hand.

"We need to get out of here," he said.

Her head was dizzy. Nothing was making sense. Why was there so much blood? Why were the mirrors broken? Who were all the dead men?

"But what about Dad?" she heard herself ask. "What about Alice and Owen?"

"They're gone Sian," Gavin said. "They're gone. It's just you and me."

She laughed a little hysterically, her eyes still gazing at her mom's chalk white face. "How can you say that?" she demanded. "This is ridiculous! Tell me it's a dream! Wake me up!" Her cheeks were wet with tears, but she didn't understand why. "Wake me up," she whispered, feeling like a single breath would shatter her.

Gavin grabbed her face, forcing her to look at him. "Sian, I swear to you, you are awake. This is not a dream."

Her whole body went cold. Gavin never lied to her. Not ever. If he said... Even if it was a dream he wouldn't lie to her. So it wasn't. It couldn't be. Her legs gave out, and she dropped to her knees.

Her sweet, funny mother was dead. Her throat had been sliced from side to side, and it gaped open like a mouth, like a laughing mouth. But her mother's face was slack and dead. Her mom was dead. It wasn't a dream. She was really dead.

A sob tore past Sian's lips as she grabbed her mom's wrist, feeling frantically for a pulse she knew wouldn't be there.

"She's gone, Sian," Gavin whispered.

"NO!!!" she wailed. "How?!!! WHY?!!!" She wanted to close her mom's throat, wanted the gruesome open smile to go away, wanted her to open her real mouth and say "I'm not really dead, sweetie. Everything's okay".

"We have to go," Gavin said, pulling Sian away from their mother's side.

Sian pushed him away, then froze. The spilled cereal. It had been Crunchy-O's. Only Owen ate Crunchy-O's.

She jumped to her feet and ran up the winding staircase two at a time.

"OWEN!!!" she screamed. "ALICE!!! WHERE ARE YOU?!!!"

No one answered. There was no sound at all except the soft pad of Gavin running behind her.

Sian scrambled over a dead man in the hallway on her way to Alice's room. The door was open, but Alice's room was empty.

"ALICE!" she screamed again, pushing back past Gavin and bolting down the hallway.

More dead men. She wasn't counting. She couldn't think outside her fear. Mom was dead. Mom was dead. Mom was dead.

There was blood on the hallway floor. There were bloody handprints on the walls. Why was there so much blood? Where was Alice? Why weren't they answering? She refused to believe they were dead. They couldn't be dead.

The wall across from Owen's door was riddled with bullet holes. There were legs in the hallway. Dead legs, but they couldn't be Owen's. He'd never wear pressed pants like those.

Sian stopped just outside the door and stared. Owen's door had been broken down. Three men lay just inside the room, oxford shirts stained red with their own blood.

And there was Owen. Splayed out on top of his trunk, gun still clutched in his hand, eyes glassy blue. There was a knife sticking out of his throat, and blood dripped sluggishly from around the knife, staining his favorite ironic t-shirt.

"Owen, oh sweet Owen." She stumbled towards him, numb and cold, ignoring Gavin's grasping fingers, ignoring his order to "leave right this minute". She had to see Owen.

She touched his face with trembling fingers. He was still warm, but he was dead. His restrained energy, his serious smile, gone, all gone.

She wanted to hug him, to tell him everything was okay. But she couldn't. He was dead. He would never again give her that look he always did when she said something stupid. He would never again beat her at chess. He was dead, and nothing was okay. Nothing would ever be okay again.

She closed her eyes in agony. He was her little brother, and she'd always protected him. She'd protected him from the bully at jiu jitsu class; she'd protected him from Uncle Frank's noggies; she'd protected him from Grandma's disgusting cod liver oil. But she had failed him this time. She hadn't been here, and he was dead.

"Alice," she gasped. "Alice! ALICE!!!"

She turned from Owen and started searching his room, but she didn't see Alice anywhere. Maybe she'd gotten away. Maybe she'd run.

Gavin grabbed Sian's hand, grip hard. "Listen to me, Sian. We have to go. Now!"

"But Dad and Grandma and Alice! We have to find them!"

"No."

"We have to! Mom is dead! Owen is dead! Don't you understand?!!"

"We have to go!" Gavin's voice was hard. "You don't understand, and I can't explain it to you. We have to go!"

"No! Not without Alice."

"Stubborn ass," Gavin hissed, pulling her out of Owen's room and past all the other bedrooms until they reached the end of the hallway.

Sian stopped breathing when she saw the doors to the master suite had been torn from their hinges. Suddenly she didn't want to go any further. She should have gone when Gavin told her to. She didn't want to go inside her parent's bedroom, but it was too late.

Gavin dragged her inside, dropping her arm just on the other side of the door. Her chest ached from holding her breath, and as soon as she saw the destruction inside the room, all her air rushed out in a terrified gasp.

Her parent's room was completely destroyed. Her mom's collection of glass horses had been shattered into millions of pieces. Her dad's framed original Jerry Uelsmann photographs had been torn from the walls and smashed into unrecognizable pieces. Everything was in chaos. It barely resembled the room Sian knew so well.

She blundered through the debris, looking for something, anything, that would tell her why this had happened. But she couldn't find a thing, just broken bits and pieces of her parent's lives.

She glanced across the room and saw Gavin, his shoulders sagging, standing in front of the walk-in closet. The double doors were hanging open, and there was blood on the closet floor.

"No," she whispered, feeling the last remnants of her hope wither away.

"Stay here," Gavin hissed as he stepped into the closet.

There was a gun in Gavin's hand, and Sian wondered vaguely where it had come from. Everything was wrong. Gavin was wrong, acting so serious and hard. The blood, the death, Mom, Owen, all wrong.

Who had killed all those men? Why had they been here in the first place? Why had they killed Mom? Why had they killed Owen? What were they looking for? Why didn't anything make sense?

Her feet moved, taking her inside the closet. It wasn't a dream. Gavin had sworn it wasn't, but it felt so unreal, so hazy, so strange. Owen dead. Sweet, red-haired Owen. Blue eyes frozen open. Blood oozing onto the floor.

Her feet kept moving without her consent, taking her further into the closet. She didn't remember it being so long. She glanced up and gasped in surprise. There was a hidden door at the end. Inside her parent's closet.

The air didn't feel like air anymore. She had to be dreaming. She had to be. Gavin wasn't freaking out. He wasn't screaming or sobbing or panicking. He was acting like it was something he'd seen before. But how could he? None of this was right. None of this was right.

She stepped closer to the hidden door, feeling like she was about to walk into a hidden world. A world of secrets and queens, a world of magic.

But instead it was a world of death. Sian couldn't move past the first dead body. She couldn't step over him, couldn't move into the hidden room she hadn't known was there.

They were all dead. Dad, Alice, Grandma. Dead. It didn't make sense. But even more so, what Sian couldn't explain, what she didn't understand, was the others. There were at least fifteen men in the secret room with them. All dead. Had Dad killed them? Her serious, studious dad? All fifteen of them? He couldn't have, he wasn't... She didn't understand.

She wanted to touch Alice, she wanted to hold her hand, move her hair out of her eyes, hug her, hold her, but she didn't. She couldn't. Alice was dead. There was too much blood on her chest for her not to be.

Crazy, independent Alice. She'd never again fill a room with her cheerful laughter. She'd never drive her pink, little roadster across the country like she'd planned. She'd never breathe... ever again.

Sian couldn't breathe either. Just standing there, staring at Alice, knowing she was dead, Sian felt like she was dying too. Every breath was shorter and shorter. Her chest heaved; her vision darkened. She couldn't breathe. She couldn't... she just couldn't.

Gavin turned just in time to catch Sian as she fell. Goddamn her for being so stubborn. He should have dragged her away as soon as he'd seen the blood. He should have thrown her over his shoulder and driven away, never looking back. As soon as he'd seen the blood he'd known. He'd known they were dead.

"Gavin," a harsh voice whispered.

His heart thudded as he lowered Sian carefully to the floor. "Grandma, you're alive!"

"Not for long, boy. Come here."

He stepped over several dead men and knelt beside her, taking her fragile hand in his own. He could see she was already near death, and he wanted to make empty promises and tell her everything would be alright, but he knew better.

"We've been betrayed," she whispered, voice cracking with pain, face twisted in anger. "Betrayed by one of our own. Find them and avenge us! You are now the head. It is your duty."

"I swear," he whispered as the life faded from her eyes. "I will not rest until they pay. I will make them all pay." She didn't hear him; she was already gone. Her hand was limp in his, and her face was slack, lacking any sign of the grandma he loved.

He closed his eyes for a minute, forcing the grief away, trying to hold on to everything Grandma had taught him. Perseverance and right were on his side. Justice would guide him, just as it always had.

He quickly checked Alice. She was dead. He'd known she was. There was no point in checking his dad. Gavin could have put his hand through the hole in his dad's chest.

He angrily swiped a tear from his cheek. Grief would do him no good. He needed anger. And righteous retribution on those who had betrayed his family. On those who had murdered them.

He searched the room, but his father's journals were gone. All the records and notes his father was in charge of as head of the family were gone. Everything was gone.

It was just him. Him and Sian. He felt a quick wave of despair. How could he avenge his family while keeping Sian safe? He glanced at her. She was still unconscious, sweet-faced, innocent, and angel-like in the soft lights of the closet. How he wished she was just a little harder, just a little meaner, had just a little more edge.

He searched one of the dead men, knowing it was futile. Only an amateur would have anything on them that would tell Gavin anything, and these men hadn't been amateurs. If they had been, his family would still be alive.

He didn't find anything. No receipts, no cards or ID's. Not even loose change. He searched them all but found nothing.

He located the special floor panel, popped it open, and pulled out the lockbox. Everything he and Sian would need was in there. His family was nothing if not prepared.

He opened the box and picked up the phone stored there. He pushed the power button, mind whirling. He had to call them. It didn't matter that one of them had betrayed them all. He didn't know who it was, and he couldn't let everyone suffer just to protect himself.

He made his way quickly through the contact list, calling everyone. Most of them answered. Some of them didn't. His words were brief and always the same.

"The house has fallen. Trust no one."

He knew he didn't have to speak in code, didn't have to overcomplicate it. But one of them, one of them, was a turncoat. And until he knew which one, he didn't know who to trust and didn't want anyone to trust anyone else.

After he'd called the last contact, he powered down the phone and put it back in the box. It was time to go. There was nothing for them here, and it wouldn't be long before they came looking for him.

He glanced around the room one last time. He'd spent so many hours here with Owen and Alice, listening and learning as his dad had taught them what it meant to be an Ellis. He'd taken his oath here, right before his first kill. He'd pledged his allegiance to the Ellis family, to justice, to the removal of corruption in all its forms.

He couldn't believe it. His father was dead. His family was dead. But he was still an Ellis. He would always be an Ellis. And now he was the Ellis head.

He cast one last glance at his dad, missing him already, missing his words of wisdom and his dry humor. He had ruled with a firm but fair hand. He had been a good leader. But someone had betrayed his trust, and Gavin would make them pay.

Chapter Two

Volume 2; Entry 112; April of 1890, **Jack Ellis***:*
Bronwen and I saw our new home for the first time today. The young town of Golden is nestled amongst the mountains like a special treat, and as soon as I saw it I knew it was perfect.

Bronwen is not yet convinced of my decision, but she is quite pregnant so I forgive her for not understanding the brilliance of it. She will eventually come around to my point of view. She always does.

The east coast cities are already too well established to accept a newcomer as a leader among them, but the West is willing and ready to accept new leadership and new blood, for indeed that is all they have.

With my lineage and fortune, we will be able to create a life for ourselves here, far away from the filthy air and oppressive politics of London.

It was dark when Sian woke. She lay in bed for a minute, head fuzzy, body aching, feeling like she had forgotten something important. She rubbed the sleep from her eyes, then gasped, remembering her terrible and vivid nightmare.

She rolled out of bed, fumbling for her lamp switch. She had to find Gavin, make sure he was okay, and then she'd tell him all about her dream and they would laugh.

Her hand hit something, but it wasn't her lamp. Something was wrong. The room didn't feel right. There was carpet under her feet not bare boards. Sian's heart dropped.

She wasn't in her room. She wasn't home. She didn't know where she was. Her fingers found a switch, and she flipped it, instantly realizing she was in some sort of hotel.

Gavin was sitting in a chair across from her, face grim and covered in shadows, gun resting on his lap.

"It wasn't a dream, was it?" she whispered, sitting back down on the bed.

"No."

"Gavin... What? Why?" Tears streamed down her cheeks. Why would anyone want to kill her family? Who would want to hurt them? They'd never hurt anyone. They were upstanding members of the community. They had been for over a hundred years.

"What's going on?" she whispered, suddenly terrified. Gavin wasn't himself. He wasn't goofy and full of laughter. He was stiff and mechanical, and he was scaring her.

"I can't explain it to you," he said, voice edged with regret. "But I need your help, Sian. I need you with me."

She didn't know what that meant and was too scared to ask.

"Someone," he said, voice infused with so much hatred she flinched. "Someone betrayed Dad. Us. All of us. Someone in our family, and I don't know who."

"Betrayed us? How?"

He shook his head and said, "That's not important. What's important is that it happened, and you and I are going to hunt them down and kill them."

"WHAT?!!" Sian screeched, recoiling in horror. How could he even suggest such a thing? They couldn't kill anyone, let alone another Ellis.

"Kill them!" Gavin snapped. "Avenge Mom, Dad, Grandma, Alice, and Owen! We have to!"

She pinched herself. It was simply too bizarre to be real. It couldn't be real. Nothing was making sense. Her entire family had been brutally murdered. Gavin was talking about betrayal and revenge. It was wrong. Everything was wrong.

"Grandma made me swear," Gavin added softly.

"Grandma?" Sian asked, feeling a burst of hope. "She's alive?"

"No," Gavin said harshly. "She's dead."

"Then how...?"

"It's not complicated!" he barked, not looking like her brother at all. "She was alive, told me to avenge them, and then she died!"

Sian swallowed a sob and stared at him, wanting to hug him, hold him tight, and tell him it was okay, just like she'd done when his favorite dog Midnight had died. But she couldn't. He wasn't Gavin. He was someone else. Someone she didn't recognize.

"Why did Dad have a hidden room?" she whispered. "Who killed all those men? Who were they?"

He shook his head in frustration. "I can't tell you. You just have to trust me. It's just you and me. We're all we have."

Sian didn't answer for a minute. Then she finally said, "But what about Uncle Danny or Alistair or Nick, Joseph..."

"No," he interrupted. "We're alone."

They'd never been alone. Not ever. There were so many Ellises, and they were always together.

"Then how... what..." she started.

"We just figure it out. It shouldn't be that hard."

She didn't believe him. She also didn't know what exactly they were going to figure out. She could tell Gavin knew more than he was saying, but he wasn't telling her, and she didn't understand why.

He was her best friend. They never kept secrets from each other. At least she hadn't ever kept a secret from him. But he had. He'd known about the hidden room. He knew what was going on. He knew why their family had died. He was keeping secrets from her.

The room suddenly felt small, and in the dim light he looked sinister, like a villain waiting to be revealed. She shuddered, folding her knees up to her chest. She wished he would trust her. She didn't have any choice; she had to trust him. He was all she had.

"They'll be looking for me," Gavin added offhandedly. "So we'll just set a trap."

"A trap?" Sian gasped. "Are you insane?"

"A trap," he repeated. "All we need is one."

"One what?"

"If we get one of the assassins, he'll tell us everything we need to know," Gavin ground out, eyes hard as diamonds and just as sharp.

Sian closed her eyes, but when she opened them Gavin's eyes were still unrecognizable. "Gavin, it's not too late," she insisted. "If you don't want to call the police, we should at least call Nick and Joseph. They'll help us. You know they will."

"No!" he said firmly.

Sian shrunk against the headboard. His tone of voice made it clear he would accept no argument, and it reminded her of their dad.

"I'm going to go get some food," he said abruptly. "You stay here. Promise me you won't leave this room."

"I won't," she whispered.

"Promise me. Pinky swear." He held out his pinky like he'd done a thousand times before.

The punishment for breaking a pinky swear was having all your toenails ripped off. It hurt terribly. She'd never felt it, but Owen had once broken a pinky swear and she had held him down while Gavin had ripped off just ONE of Owen's toenails. Owen had screamed like a girl, and he'd never, ever broken a pinky swear again.

She reached out her hand slowly, knowing if their pinkies touched she wouldn't leave the room until he told her she could.

"I swear," she whispered, wrapping her pinky with his.

"I'll be back," he said. Suddenly the hardness left his eyes, replaced by grief and sadness. "Oh Sian," he whispered. "I'm so sorry." He hugged her tightly, and she clung to him, wishing she could go back to this morning, before all this, and make them all run away with her.

"I wish..."

"What?" she asked.

"Nothing."

Suddenly he was gone, and the air around her felt cold. As soon as the door closed behind him, Sian dropped to the floor and wept.

They were dead. Her entire family was dead. All of them. Except for Gavin. Her best friend. Her partner in crime. Her big brother. She needed him, but he was so altered, so changed, it was like he wasn't himself at all.

Gavin sighed heavily as he walked down the motel's dim, long hallway. The walls were filthy; the carpet was stained and bare; there were no surveillance cameras, no security whatsoever. This was the kind of motel someone stayed at when they didn't want to be found or when they had a shady business deal going on.

There was enough cash in the lockbox for them to stay anywhere they wished for as long as they wanted. Furthermore Gavin had access to over a dozen accounts with plenty of funds, but he preferred staying under the radar. Whoever this was would expect him to hide in the style he was accustomed to. No one would expect Gavin to slum.

Normally he'd never leave Sian alone in a place like this, but he needed a minute. If she kept looking at him with her questioning, confused eyes, he'd break and tell her everything. Their family had seen enough betrayal today, and he wasn't going to add his to it. She would just have to trust him.

He'd get food, more weapons, contact some of his people, and try to get a lead on where the assassins had come from and why. He wished Grandma had lived just a minute longer so she could have told him something, anything, just more than what she had.

They had never trained for anything like this. Not really. There was only one of him, and who knew how many of them. He wished he could trust someone besides Sian. He had family a plenty, but he didn't know who he could trust, and he didn't want to put Sian in danger by trusting the wrong person. He could call Nick; he knew he could. But what about Nick's wife, Nick's brother, Nick's mom? No. He'd have to figure it out on his own.

Volume 2; Entry 138, **Jack Ellis**

In the short time I have been here I have already compiled a list of those I have found full of corruption. In my naivety I thought the corruptness of such a small town would be less than London or New York. I failed to account for the political structure of this land.

A land ran by the people, for the people. Only it isn't. Wealthy politicians make promise after promise of all they will do for those voting for them, but once they are in office they do not carry through on their promises. They do not protect their people or fight for their people or even care about their suffering. I am stunned by how much it truly resembles the corruption of my own country.

It is hard to know how to proceed. I am no longer part of a larger group. I am no longer a spoke in a wheel. I am but one man, and the task before me is daunting.

Ah, but what a foolish man I am, still blinded by my father's archaic rules and beliefs. Bronwen is with me, and she is more valuable than any brother I have and any man I have ever met. With her by my side, as my partner, I am capable of anything.

It felt as if Sian wept for hours. She couldn't stop seeing her mom's face, white and slack, bloody smile underneath. She couldn't stop seeing Owen's glassy blue eyes. She couldn't stop seeing Alice's crumpled body on the floor. Or the hole in her dad's chest. Or the blood on her grandma's head.

But that wasn't all. Questions spun through her head. So many questions. There was the hidden room she'd never known existed. The one Gavin knew was there. There was the gun lying limply in Alice's dead hand. She'd never seen such a ridiculous gun, so brightly colored. Teal and pink. Alice's two favorite colors.

Alice was only seventeen. Or she had been. She was dead now. She wasn't anything. But she had been there in that room, the room Sian hadn't known existed, and she'd had a gun in her hand. And somehow Sian knew, she just knew, Alice had killed at least some of those men.

When had Alice learned to shoot? Sian supposed it made sense. When Sian was younger she'd gone shooting all the time with her dad. She could still feel her dad's warm hands close over hers as he'd taught her how to aim.

"Squeeze the trigger, Sian girl. Don't jerk. Squeeze."

He'd let go of her, stepping back, and Sian had squinted down the sight the way he'd taught her. The target had blurred for a moment, then sharpened, and Sian squeezed.

The air exploded around her, and she squealed, almost dropping the gun.

"Did you see that?!" Gavin yelled excitedly from behind her. "She hit the bull's eye! First time!"

"Good job, Sian," Dad had said, voice pleased. "Again."

Sian shook her head, clearing the memory and trying to remember Alice with a gun in her hands. Suddenly an image of five-year-old Alice resurfaced. Just as brash and loud as she was at seventeen, holding a pistol almost as big as she was.

"Did you see that, Daddy?" little Alice crowed. "I almost hit the target!"

Sian, Owen, and Gavin had laughed and moved off to play their own game of take out the sniper. Sian frowned. When had she stopped going shooting with them? At some point her dad had just stopped taking her. There were an awful lot of things he had stopped taking her to. Her jiu jitsu classes. The fencing club. To observe criminal court. She'd even stopped participating in the family games.

Why? Why had she stopped? Why hadn't she asked why? But she remembered now. She hadn't questioned him because he'd filled her life with so many other things. He'd purchased her a camera and snowshoes and sent her to a month long gourmet cooking course.

She was terrible at cooking, but photography had seemed to come to her naturally, so her dad bought her books and computer equipment and enrolled her in course after course after course. He'd even sponsored her blog before she'd started making money on her own, not that she'd needed it.

All the Ellises had trust funds that would support them their entire life, even if they lived to be a hundred and fifty. But that didn't stop them from working. The Ellises were vital, hard-working members of the community; they always had been.

She stared at the stained carpet, trying to remember how she'd gotten here. What did photography and trust funds have to do with her family being murdered?

The gun. The gun in Alice's hand. Alice's gun. How many of those men had Alice killed? And why did that make Sian so sad?

Alice was the wild one, the crazy one, the one who came up with ideas like "let's all go skinny dipping in Clear Creek" even though it was snowing and only fifteen degrees out.

But a killer? Was Alice a killer? She'd used the gun, Sian was sure of it. She'd killed at least some of the men in that hidden room. And Owen must have killed the men in his doorway. But of course he had. Owen was a killer shot. She just hadn't known he could kill.

Suddenly Sian wasn't sure of anything. If someone had asked her yesterday, she wouldn't have thought either of her siblings had the ability to kill someone. She'd have laughed at the very thought. Why would they need to kill anyone anyway? That kind of thing only happened in movies, not real life.

The idea that she didn't really know them, or hadn't known them, frightened her. How could she not have known them? They were her family. She loved them; they loved her. Didn't they?

She felt like there was three of her, all arguing with herself. One was weeping, asking "why" over and over and over, one wanted to hunt Gavin down and beat the answers out of him, and the other one was insisting that Ellises trusted each other, always had each other's backs, and it didn't matter what Gavin had done, he needed her.

She squeezed her head between her hands, wanting to scream. She needed someone to talk to. Someone who loved her. She looked at the phone by the bed. Gavin hadn't said she couldn't call anyone. It had been implied, but there had been no crossing of the pinkies, no swearing on the toes.

She glanced toward the door. She didn't know how long it had been or when he would be back. But she had to know what was going on.

She picked up the receiver, hearing her own harsh breath, and called her cousin Louise. Louise answered after three rings. "Hello?"

"Louise?" Sian whispered.

"Sian? Is that you? Where are you?"

Sian's breath caught. How did Louise know she was anywhere other than home? Why had that been the first question she'd asked? Why was her voice so stern and worried?

"What's going on?" Sian asked, tears making her vision blurry.

"Sian, tell me where you are. I'll come get you."

"What's going on?"

"Sian!" Louise snapped, no sign of her usual cheerfulness. "Where the hell are you?!"

Sian hung up the phone and crawled onto the bed. She wrapped her arms around her knees and stared at the wall. Something was very wrong, and no one would tell her what. Gavin said to trust him, but he didn't trust her. He'd never told her about the secret room. Everyone else knew. Alice and Owen knew, but she didn't. Gavin didn't trust her; how could she trust him?

A car honked outside, and Sian jumped. What if that was them? The men who'd killed her family? What if they wanted to kill her too? She crept silently to the window and peeked through the curtain. There were only two people in the parking lot, and they looked likc strung-out druggies not like oxford-shirt-wearing assassins.

Sian dropped the curtain and glanced at the clock. Gavin had been gone for such a long time. At least she thought he had; she hadn't checked the time when he left. What if he never came back? He clearly didn't trust her. Maybe he'd left her here to rot. But why would he do that? He wouldn't. He loved her. He was her best friend.

Sian tried to shake off her panic. Gavin would never leave her. Not ever. He was her big brother. He'd always protected her. And there were no assassins hunting her down. She was fine. But it was too quiet. So quiet all she could hear were her own strangled sobs. She fumbled for the remote and turned on the TV.

The local news was playing, and in the background Sian's home was burning.

"I'm here on scene at the ancestral Ellis mansion," the pretty newscaster said. "As you can see behind me the Ellis home is on fire. Local firefighters are working hard to put out the blaze, and at this time it is unknown as to whether any of the Ellis family is inside."

The newscaster paused here, as if to silently mourn the unknown Ellis casualties, then she smiled cheerfully and went on. "The Ellis family has been a solid part of our community ever since Jack and Bronwen Ellis immigrated to Golden in 1890. You'll find members of the Ellis family all over Golden and surrounding areas, taking part in town leadership, education, law enforcement, the judicial system, and the community at large. Our hearts go out to the Ellis family tonight." She paused again. "We hope..."

Sian pressed the mute button and watched in horror as her home burned. She was certain Gavin had started the fire. She didn't know if that meant he was trying to cover up their murders or what. She didn't know anything. He wouldn't tell her.

She fought the urge to scream. If he didn't come back soon she was walking out the door, toenails be damned. She didn't owe him anything.

She started pacing, anything to help push off the fear. She knew she wouldn't leave the room. He was her family. He may not trust her, but she loved him, and she would never abandon him.

She was pacing the length of the room when the door started to open. She swallowed a scream, then grabbed the bedside lamp and scrambled silently over to the door. She stood there just beside it, waiting and holding the lamp high.

"Gavin," she gasped in relief as he pushed the door open and stepped into the room. The lamp dropped from her hands, shattering on the floor in front of him.

"Damn, Sian," he laughed. "You just broke the damn lamp."

"I don't care about the lamp! Where've you been?!"

"Out." He smiled at her, and she could see the relief in his eyes. He hadn't been sure she would be here. He should have known she would never leave him.

"I got some pizza," he said, holding the box out to her.

Her stomach growled, and she grimaced. How could she be hungry after what she'd seen today? The thought of eating made her stomach roll, but then it growled and complained.

"You have to eat," Gavin said. "We have a long night ahead of us."

"Did you burn the house?"

"Yes."

"Why?" She knew they were already dead, but the idea of them burning, of their skin turning black and cracking away just like a bunny on a spit, made her sick.

"Because," he said, face completely blank. "Anyway, eat. I'll be right back."

He sat the box on the table and left the room. She wanted to stop him, to scream for him not to leave her. She didn't ever want to be alone again. It was too frightening. She didn't trust herself.

He soon returned with a large duffle bag and several shopping bags. "Got you some clothes," he said. "And a toothbrush."

It was then that she realized her clothes were covered in dried blood. She swallowed a gag. Her mom's blood was on her. Touching her. Coating her skin.

"I have to shower," she mumbled, grabbing a bag and running into the bathroom.

Gavin watched her go with a sigh. It would be so much easier if he could just cut her loose, drop her off somewhere safe and leave her be. But he couldn't. He'd never been able to. She was his best friend. Always had been. He could still remember peeking into her crib and thinking, "That's my baby sister. Mine. Protect."

She wasn't cut out for this, but she'd have to learn because he'd lost nearly his entire family today, and he wasn't letting her go. He would protect her, he would keep her safe, and he would kill the scum who had killed his family. He would make them pay. He would take their blood. He would destroy them.

He was Gavin Ellis. It would be easy for him. All he had to do was bait the trap and wait.

Sian sobbed helplessly as she ripped off her clothes and threw them on the floor. Her mom was dead. Dead. Burned and dead.

She stumbled into the shower, turning the heat up and standing under the pounding spray. She should have hugged her mom this morning before they left instead of sneaking out the back door. She should have said she loved her; she should've hugged Owen and Alice, Grandma and Dad. She would never hug them again, and she didn't understand why.

She missed them already. She missed Grandma's soft hand pats, Dad's approving nods, Mom's warm hugs, Owen's shoulder bumps, and Alice's whirlwind cheek kisses. She would never touch them again, never hear their voices again. Never... never... never...

She let the water pour down on her, trying desperately to move the puzzle pieces into place, but she didn't have them all. She only had a few of them, and they didn't make a whole picture.

All she knew was that someone wanted her family dead. They had killed everyone but Gavin and her. Gavin wouldn't tell her why, but he said he needed her help to avenge their family. That was all she knew, but that was all she needed to know. Someone had hurt her family, and they would pay. Just like that damn bully who hadn't left Owen alone.

She turned off the water, dried herself, and pulled on the clothes Gavin had bought her. There was no blood on her skin now, but she still didn't feel clean. She'd touched their dead skin. How could she ever feel clean again?

She stared at herself in the mirror, feeling a hundred years older. Then she pulled her hair into a ponytail and opened the door.

"Tell me what I need to do," she said.

Relief flooded Gavin's face, and he grinned at her. "Eat first," he said. "Then we'll talk plans."

"So," Gavin said after they had demolished the pizza, "there are a group of assassins somewhere in town, assuming they're still here."

Sian paled. "Assassin" on its own was a terrible sounding word. "Group of assassins" made her want to crawl into the tub and hide. Why would anyone send a "group" of assassins after her family? It didn't make sense.

"I'm guessing the job isn't done until I'm dead too," he added. "So logically, we lure them in, snatch one, and get the information we need from him."

"Logically?" Sian muttered. "Logically? What part of that seems logical to you?"

"The part where we get what we need."

"Oh. I see."

This was definitely not the same Gavin who played tennis with her. Or Egyptian rat killer. Or rode around with her finding abandoned places to photograph for her blog. This was not that Gavin.

A memory tugged at her. They were playing a game of eliminate the dictator. Gavin and she were one team; there were three other teams comprised of Owen and the other Ellis cousins. The team to eliminate the dictator first would win.

Gavin and she had hunkered down in the old carriage house, and Gavin had laid out his plan. His face had looked a lot like it did right now. Confident, hard, and committed.

They had won that game. They always did. Gavin had never lost a game of eliminate the dictator, and they weren't going to lose tonight.

Someone had hurt their family, and they needed to pay. No one, absolutely no one, hurt the Ellises and got away with it.

Chapter Three

Volume 2; Entry 157; **Jack Ellis***:*

Today I am the proud father of a son, Henry Jack Ellis. I do hope to be a better father than my own. Perhaps someday my father and I will mend our rift, but I fear our thoughts on the future are just too different.

We broke ground on our home the same day Henry was born. I acknowledge the symbolism of such an action, and I felt the power it generated when I thrust my shovel into the virgin soil.

Soon my son will live in a house built by my own hands, metaphorically of course. With every stone put in place, my hold on the town leaders grows stronger and stronger. Before long, they will be coming to me for everything, even advice on how to button their coats.

After Gavin explained his plan, Sian just stared at him. After a minute she said, "Surely there's a better way?"

He shrugged. "The thing is I've never tried to draw in an assassin before, so I'm kind of winging it. I think it'll work though."

He handed her a slim 9mm and three spare clips full of bullets and asked, "You remember how to shoot, right?"

"Yes," she muttered. "Can you really forget how to shoot?"

"It's just you haven't gone with us in a long time," he said, his tone adding a question at the end, like he just wanted to verify she actually remembered how.

She felt a flash of resentment and snapped, "And whose fault is that?! Dad stopped taking me. No one asked me to go! I didn't even remember Alice could shoot until today!"

Gavin's eyes slid away from hers, and she knew he was hiding more things from her. He had been hiding things from her all this time. He'd been lying to her face. She wanted to knock his teeth out. Or rip off all his toenails. Their pinkies may not have ever crossed, but it was implied. Ellises didn't lie to each other.

"I remember how to shoot!" she growled, feeling angry. And she did remember. She could still feel the weight of a gun in her hand, still feel the way the trigger depressed, still feel the brief moment of elation when her bullet hit the spot she'd aimed at.

He shrugged and handed her some slim, black tubes with retractable keychain cords attached to them. "These are mace; just aim and push the trigger."

She rolled her eyes. He obviously didn't believe her, but she did remember. She could still hit the bull's eye, and she would prove it. She shook her head in disgust. What exactly would she prove it on? An assassin? It's not like she actually wanted to kill someone.

She took the maces and hooked them to her pants, testing the retractable keychain lines. Then he pressed a knife into her hand, and she shuddered. She hadn't touched a knife since she'd gone hunting with her dad and he'd made her skin the rabbit they'd killed.

There was just something about taking a creature's life and then eating it that made Sian sick. She understood it. She understood it was no different than eating beef or chicken. But she had seen the rabbit when it was alive. And she had seen it die. She had killed it.

But she wasn't hunting a rabbit today. She was hunting a killer, a group of killers. She may not have ever killed anyone, but she understood how, and today she understood why. She took the knife and slid it onto her belt.

"I need you, Sian," Gavin said, eyes serious. "You're all I have." She nodded shakily. "I know you don't like to kill things," he said. "But this isn't like killing a fish or a rabbit or a deer. This is survival. These people want us dead. They killed our family. We have to kill them. We have to."

"I know," she whispered. And she really did. She'd kill as many people as she needed to to protect Gavin. She'd kill the entire world if she had to.

"Do you need me to go over the plan one more time?" he asked. She shook her head. "Are you sure?"

"I'm sure."

"Okay, let's go."

He hugged her tightly, resting his head on hers. "I need you. You've got this. You're an Ellis. You can do this. It's in your blood."

She nodded. She wasn't altogether convinced she could do it, but she couldn't fail Gavin. She wouldn't.

They left the motel and climbed into a car Sian had never seen before. She didn't ask where he had gotten it; she didn't want to know.

She didn't speak as Gavin drove across town towards a popular bar, but she wanted to scream at him. She wanted to tell him how stupid his plan was, how stupid he was, but she couldn't.

"Why can't we call Uncle Danny?" she finally asked.

"No."

"But why not?"

She heard him sigh, then he said, "Listen, I can't explain it to you; you just have to believe me. Someone in the family is trying to kill us. Do you really want me to just pick one from a hat, call them, and hope they're not the one who wants us dead?"

"No, but I don't understand why you think someone in the family is trying to kill us. That's insane!"

"You just have to trust me."

"You keep saying that! Why won't YOU trust ME?!"

"I do," he whispered. "Believe me I do, but I can't tell you anything. I'm sorry."

Sian stared at the window and fought the tears that wanted to spill. Everything was broken, and she didn't know how to fix it. Yesterday she'd been Sian Ellis, beloved daughter of Edward and Silvia Ellis. She'd had three wonderful siblings, an amazing grandma, and an entire slew of relatives whom she loved and adored. Gavin was her best friend in the whole world. Louise was second. Sian loved, and she was loved, and everything was perfect. Nothing was out of place.

But now... Everything was wrong. Everything she'd known yesterday was shadowed by the lies of today, the hidden room, the guns, Gavin's insistence on betrayal and revenge. Nothing she'd thought could be true now. Nothing.

Gavin parked on the street and stared at the bar. Sian could tell by the set of his shoulders he wasn't completely convinced his plan would work. It was the same way his shoulders looked when they went to play tennis.

"Let's just run," she suggested earnestly. "We can go to Canada or Mexico."

"I can't."

"Why not?"

He made an exasperated noise and said, "Because I can't, Sian! I have responsibilities! I have... And anyway, Grandma..."

"Right," she whispered, dread filling her. "You made a pinky swear. So let's do this." Sian's heart was hammering so hard she almost didn't hear his soft reply.

"Love you, Sian."

"Love you too, you jerk."

He chuckled softly and handed her a wig and sunglasses. "I always thought you'd look good as a brunette."

She cringed. "Did you hear about the brunette and the lawyer?"

"No; tell me after we do this."

"Yeah, sure." She pulled the wig over her hair and pushed the sunglasses on. She yanked the big grey hoodie he'd given her earlier over her head and tugged it down so it covered her gun.

"I'll go in," Gavin said, "and make a scene, then leave. Follow me out."

"I know the plan."

"I know; I was just saying."

"I know the damn plan, Gavin!"

"Okay." He swallowed hard.

"Don't worry," she said, faking a smile. "We're Ellises. We always have each other's back."

He nodded and stepped from the car. She watched as his posture went from tense to wobbly and goofy, like he'd just drank five beers in one sitting. He tossed her a wink, then pushed open the bar door and walked inside.

Sian waited for one minute, then followed him into the bar, hood pulled low over her head, sunglasses perched on her nose. She sat at the end of the bar, far away from Gavin, ordered a Coors, flashing the bartender her new ID, and watched Gavin play his role.

"They won't let me into the house!" he exclaimed to the crowd of people gathered around him. "And they won't tell me anything! I can't get a hold of Dad or Mom or anyone!"

Someone handed him a beer, and he tossed it back effortlessly. "I'm so freaked out," he said, wiping his brow. "Surely they got out, but where are they?"

The Ellises ran the town, so Gavin's story didn't make a lot of sense, not really. But no one questioned a word he said. He was an Ellis after all.

"Did you call the fire chief?" one of the men asked.

"I tried, but he won't return my calls." Which was ridiculous; the fire chief was one of their cousins. Gavin leaned his head on the bar. "God... I can't believe any of this."

"What about Nick?" somebody else suggested. "Surely he would know something."

"I can't reach him either," Gavin muttered. "I can't... Goddamn it's hot in here." He suddenly stood. "I've got to go. I'll go out there again. I'll make them let me in."

"Let me drive you," someone said.

Gavin waved him off. "No, I can't... I need to be alone."

"Are you sure you can drive?" the bartender asked uncertainly. "I don't think you should." People didn't normally tell Ellises what to do. Ellises told other people what to do.

"I'm fine," Gavin said, infusing a bit of steel into his voice. "I only had one beer. I'll be alright."

The crowd parted as Gavin headed for the door, and they offered him empty condolences and reassurances as he went. Sian could tell they all believed the Ellis family was dead. If they weren't, someone would have said so by now.

Sian watched Gavin walk out the door and counted to fifteen, trying to pretend it was just a game of guard the queen. When fifteen seconds were up, and everyone had returned to their conversations and their drinks, she stood and followed him, hand wrapped tightly around her mace.

*Volume 8; Entry 157, **Jack Ellis***

Henry turned six today. He was very pleased with the knife I commissioned especially for him. Bronwen less so. I told her she could not keep him a boy forever; it is time he started learning to be a man. An Ellis man.

She disagreed, and we fought heavily about it for a while. Finally, after I promised that I would commission knives for all of our children, not just the boys and that I would train them all the same, Bronwen kissed me sweetly on the cheek and told me I am a wise man. Sometimes I wonder which of us leads the other. Perhaps it is both, but I cannot be angry. She is so clever and wise; I am fortunate to have kept her.

Henry and I went out hunting and found a rabbit. I was impressed how closely Henry watched me. He is a quick learner. I will wait a little longer yet to explain to him our place in society. After all, as Bronwen said, he is still just a child.

Gavin fought the urge to look behind him. He'd played his part, and if he'd done it well it wouldn't be long before something happened. Probably. He was just guessing. For all he knew he'd wander the city for an hour and end up going back to the motel empty handed.

He could actually feel Sian somewhere behind him, and it took the edge off his fear. He'd never been scared before, and it made him feel a little ashamed. His dad wouldn't be scared. His dad would be roaring around town, throwing people up against walls until he got the answers he needed, but that had never been Gavin's style.

He walked slowly down Washington Street. It was late, and not that many people were still out, but the few who recognized him stared at him in shock.

"That's Gavin Ellis!" he heard as he passed.

"I heard they were all dead, but he must not have been there."

"I heard a rumor both he and Sian weren't there," someone else said.

"Then where's Sian?"

"I don't know, but Gavin looks like shit."

"What do you think he's doing?"

He was trolling. He was trolling for scum. He paused in front of an Ellis building, feeling a surge of grief. He remembered the day his dad had taken him downtown and showed him all the buildings they owned.

"Your great-great-great grandpa Jack was an entrepreneur," his dad had said. "But he was also a philanthropist. He believed in creating a community where everyone could prosper."

He'd taken Gavin upstairs and showed him the special crest his great-great-great grandpa had had designed and stamped on every single building he'd built.

"He built a legacy we can be proud of. A legacy we carry on every day," his dad had said, tracing the emblem with his finger.

Gavin leaned his forehead against the cold glass. His grandpa's legacy was falling down around his ears. There was no way Gavin would ever be able to bring the family back from this.

The Ellises had always been the virtuous, upright cornerstone of the community, the unquestionable leaders, the straight arrows, the incorruptible foundation. Jack had made them so. He'd dedicated his life to making the Ellises great.

But now there would always be a shadow on the Ellis family, a whiff of scandal, conspiracy, question. From this point forward Gavin would no longer be above reproach. His entire family would no longer be above reproach.

He felt a wave of depression followed by hot rage. He wouldn't let them get away with it. He wouldn't let them steal that from his family. He would find a way to stop them.

He moved forward again, walking slowly, then turned down a side alley. He heard the slight scrape of shoes behind him, and he grinned. Even professionals could be sloppy.

He carefully positioned himself along one side of the alley so he was only visible from one rooftop, and he kept an eye on the visible roof as he walked. If someone was up there they were hiding very well.

The problem with a trap was he was exposing himself in a way he'd never normally do. He was vulnerable, and that's why he needed Sian.

He knew someone was behind him, and he waited impatiently for them to try something or simply to shoot him in the back. He cringed, wishing he'd thought of that. He shrugged mentally. He couldn't think of everything, and if they were going to shoot him, they'd have probably done it by now.

He ambled towards the mouth of the alley, stumbling slightly, then turned around with a wobbly spin. He laughed softly, gazing at the five men dressed in button up shirts and pressed pants.

"Just five?" Gavin asked. "Really?"

He glanced behind him, certain he was missing someone or something, but he wasn't. At least not that he could see. He wasn't sure whether to be offended or amused.

"Five?" he asked again.

"What'd you expect?" the leader asked with a heavy English accent. "A goddamn army?"

"Yeah," Gavin said with a laugh.

"Sorry to disappoint," the leader said, moving to pull his gun from his waistband.

He wasn't fast enough though. Gavin pulled his own gun first, and the leader was dead before he even raised his gun. And so was everyone else. Except for one man. The one man Gavin left standing.

"I'm Gavin Ellis," Gavin snarled. "You should've brought a goddamn army." He shot the remaining man in his right hand, knocking his gun to the ground. Flesh and blood spewed onto the alley behind him, and the man screamed in pain, grabbing his hand, and pressing it to his chest.

Gavin walked towards the man, keeping his gun trained on his heart. "You and I are going to have a little talk," Gavin said.

"Sorry mate," the man gasped out.

Gavin leaped forward, but it was too late. The man let go of his bleeding hand, popped something into his mouth, and swallowed it.

Gavin tackled him, knowing he had only minutes at best. He blocked the man's sloppy left handed knife thrust and ripped the knife from his hand, using it to pin the man's hand to the ground. Then Gavin punched him in the jaw, knocking his head into the filthy pavement.

Ignoring the man's cries of pain, Gavin quickly straddled him and laid his own knife to the man's throat.

"Who sent you?!" Gavin demanded. "Why? Where're the others? What do you want?"

The man laughed roughly. "You're Gavin Ellis; figure it out."

Gavin punched him in the face again. "Were you there?" he growled. "Were you one of the ones?"

The man's face had started twitching, but he still smiled widely and drawled, "I slit your bitch mother's throat."

Gavin's vision turned red, and he slammed his elbow into the man's open mouth, bashing his head into the ground again and again.

He knew he needed answers, but he couldn't think. This man had broken into Gavin's house and killed his mom. He'd slit her throat to the bone. He'd killed her.

Gavin wanted to cut him into tiny pieces. He was going to die anyway, but that didn't mean Gavin couldn't hurt him on the way out.

The man suddenly started convulsing; body shaking under Gavin's weight. Then his eyes grew wide, and he began to cough violently.

Gavin raised his hand to punch him again, to destroy what was left of his face. He wouldn't get any answers now, so he'd just beat him to death and be done with it. But he couldn't. He couldn't hit him, not like this.

In the shadows of a dumpster, Sian cried silently. Gavin had killed those four men so efficiently, so easily, like he'd done it a hundred times before. And maybe he had. Maybe he'd killed hundreds and hundreds of people. Maybe they all had.

Who were they? Her family? How had she not really known them? She'd lived with them for twenty-four years. Her mom had tucked her in at night, sang her nursery rhymes, taught her the difference between a sports bra and a push-up bra.

Grandma used to sit in front of the fire and comb and braid Sian's hair, all the while telling her stories about the grandpa Sian had never met.

Sian had stayed up late at night telling Owen stories about an evil white witch and a magical lion. Alice had listened to the stories and decided the white witch should be good instead of bad. Sian and she had argued about it endlessly.

Had they all been killing people behind her back? And why? No; she didn't believe it. It was just a fluke. Alice was good with a gun, so what? Sian was good with a gun. Gavin had killed four men without blinking, so what?

They had been going to kill him. She'd seen the guns in their hands.

She watched as Gavin subdued the last man. Gavin was yelling at him, asking him questions, but Sian couldn't hear the man's answers. She saw Gavin's face turn white, she saw him raise his arm and slam it into the man's face. Somehow she knew he was going to pummel the man to death, right here in this back alley, but then Gavin stopped.

The man was convulsing and coughing, writhing on the ground beneath Gavin. Gavin hissed, his face changing from rage to disgust, and pushed to his feet.

That's when she saw the other men. She'd been watching Gavin, and they'd snuck up behind him. He'd trusted her, and she'd failed him.

Her gun was already in her hand, and she raised it. She wouldn't lose him, not Gavin. She couldn't. Even if that meant she had to kill.

Everything slowed as she sighted down the barrel on the closest man's head. She squeezed the trigger, slowly. The alley exploded. She watched blood burst from the man's head. She watched him drop to the ground, dead.

At the sound of her gunfire, Gavin spun, gun in hand, dodging another assassin's fist. Sian shot again, killing another man and another. It didn't matter that they were human. They were the enemy. They were trying to take her brother from her, and she wouldn't let them.

After killing five men she looked down her barrel again, trying to sight another, but she couldn't find one. Panic pulsed through her; where had they gone? Had she lost?

"Sian, it's done," Gavin said softly, standing right beside her.

She jerked towards his voice, and he stopped her, wrapping his warm hand over hers and bringing her gun down.

"It's done, Sian. It's okay. We have to go."

"Did we get one?"

"No."

"Oh." Sian heard the despair in Gavin's voice and wished she could make it better. She didn't understand how they hadn't gotten one. There had been at least fifteen of them. Surely they hadn't killed all of them.

Gavin slipped Sian's gun back into her holster, took her hand, and led her away. It was a good thing he was so familiar with the streets. He knew which way the police would come from once the shots had been reported, and he knew the fastest way to get back to their parked car.

Sian didn't speak as he pulled her behind him. She'd saved his life. He'd been so angry, so angry and so upset to lose his man that he hadn't heard the others approaching. He should have known they wouldn't just send five.

He'd failed. Miserably. He hadn't captured a single one. But he had learned some things. One, they were English. He hadn't expected that and didn't know what it meant, but he was certain it wasn't good. Two, they were serious about their work. Committed. Zealots. Only people who were more scared of their "employers" than death took a suicide pill to avoid any type of failure. Three, they hadn't intended to kill him. If they had, he would be dead. They had intended to take him alive.

He frowned as he shoved Sian into the car and got in the other side. Why did they want him alive? That didn't make any sense. They hadn't made any effort to take his dad alive. This whole thing was getting messier and messier by the minute.

He glanced as Sian as he drove towards the motel. She hadn't said a word; she was clearly in shock.

He remembered his first kill. There had been a moment when he'd freaked out, wondering what he'd done. He'd stared at the man and his broken neck and nearly screamed, knowing he'd been the one to break it.

He'd done it because his father had told him to. He'd done it to belong, to be part of the Ellises. If he'd known then what he knew now he would have grabbed Sian and run the other way. But he hadn't.

Instead he'd reminded himself of his father's lessons. "Corruption within the government leads to corruption on the city streets. A corrupt person is no better than a rabid dog. They both need to be put down."

Gavin had believed him then, and he still believed him. Corruption was unacceptable. But that wasn't the problem here. This was a different issue all together. He wasn't killing the corrupt; he wasn't killing the dirty or the scum or the morally bankrupt. He was killing for revenge.

Chapter Four

Volume 22; Entry 53; **Jack Ellis***:*

My son William left for San Francisco today. He is but sixteen; however, he is as much a man as he will ever be. I gave him enough money to fund a small army and sent him with a small contingent of men who also wanted to migrate further West. I paid one man very well to guard William surreptitiously with the understanding that if he neglects his duty, I will hunt him down myself.

Once again Bronwen made it very clear she is not pleased with my methods, but the truth is William is unfit to carry the Ellis name. He tends towards softness and is easily corrupted by all manner of people. It will be easier for us all if he is gone.

Henry, however, is progressing nicely. He has handled several jobs for me lately, and his style, although lacking my finesse, is quite efficient. We are traveling to Denver later this week to handle a few problems there.

The West has grown much in the twenty years since I arrived, and I am sometimes shocked to see the changes that have come and the corruptions that have followed. It saddens me to realize that given enough time Denver will be no different than London. A corrupt city with newer buildings and slightly less coal smoke.

"What happened?" Sian asked when they were once again inside their motel room.

"What do you mean?"

"That wasn't the plan."

Gavin shrugged. "Sometimes plans don't go like they're planned."

Sian grabbed her head and squeezed, trying to make the buzzing go away. "Gavin."

"Yes?"

"What happened?"

"He took a suicide pill."

She glared at him. "Like in a spy movie?"

"Yeah."

"Why? Why would he do that?"

"He didn't want to talk to me."

"Are you seriously saying he killed himself so he wouldn't talk to you, even though he knew that those other guys were coming?!"

"That's what I'm saying."

"This is stupid. I'm calling Uncle Danny!"

"No!" Gavin jumped past her and ripped the phone from the wall. "You can't call anyone!"

"Gavin!" she snapped. "Be real! Uncle Danny loves us! For crying out loud, he taught us to fish! He's helping Alice restore her roadster! I meet him for coffee and scones once a week! He's... HE'S UNCLE DANNY!!"

"SOMEONE WANTS US DEAD!!!" Gavin yelled back. "Why can't you get that through your thick skull?!"

She stared at him in shock. She'd never heard Gavin yell, not once. His face was a mask of rage, and for the first time in her life she was truly scared of him. He looked like her brother, but he wasn't.

"Damn it, Sian!" Gavin snapped. "You have to trust me. Don't leave this room; you pinky swore!"

He turned on his heel and went into the bathroom, slamming the door behind him. Sian watched him go, feeling like her entire world had been turned upside down.

She opened the window, gulping in the fresh air and staring out at Clear Creek in the distance. She'd only fished in Clear Creek once because Uncle Danny preferred quieter spots and high mountain lakes.

She'd gone fishing because Uncle Danny loved to fish, but she just didn't have the patience to cast and sit there, holding the pole and waiting, waiting, waiting. She usually ended up wandering off and exploring.

The one time she'd caught a fish, Uncle Danny had insisted she kill and gut it herself. She'd lost her lunch in the bushes, and he'd never taken her fishing again.

She'd remembered thinking that even as he'd patted her back and told her everything was okay that his eyes had seemed disappointed. She'd wanted to gut the fish, she'd wanted to do it for him, but even thinking about it now made her want to gag.

He'd laugh if she told him she'd killed a man tonight. More than one. Maybe five; she hadn't counted. It had happened so fast. She'd acted on instinct, out of pure terror and the need to protect Gavin.

It scared her how easy it had been, how simple, like somehow she'd always known how to kill, how to take a life. It really had been frighteningly similar to a game of guard the queen. Gavin had been the queen, and the assassins had been... well, the assassins.

But it hadn't been a game. It hadn't been a pretend kill. It had been a real kill. Several real kills. With real blood and real death. They hadn't just stood up after she left and gone on about their day. They were still lying on the alley filth, their blood permanently staining the ground. And they were dead. They would never see their families again. Just like her.

She watched a drunken couple cross the street, hanging onto each other and laughing wildly. She wished she could laugh. She wished she could feel anything other than anger and fear.

Gavin was right. Someone did want them dead. She just didn't believe it was someone in their family. There wasn't a family in the world that was as tight as the Ellises.

Gavin stood under the hot water and pretended the tears rolling down his cheeks were water spray. Men didn't cry. Men shouldered responsibility and moved on. Especially Ellis men.

But they were dead. They were all dead, and he couldn't save them; he hadn't saved them. It was too late to save them. He slipped to the shower floor and rocked back and forth, his heart hurting so badly he wanted to rip it from his chest.

He hadn't been there to protect them. It was his duty to protect them, and he had failed. He was the head of the Ellis line, but he wasn't fit. He was weak; he was a failure; he was totally screwed.

He sobbed silently, trying to push every memory of his family away, but he couldn't. He felt his mom's hand on his shoulder as she pushed him towards the kitchen table and made him hot cocoa after a difficult kill. He remembered Alice passing him her special scrapbook in the hallway so he could see all the news clippings of the Ellis family kills. He remembered arguing with Owen over which knife grip was most effective. Stupid things really, inconsequential moments out of his life, but they kept flashing through his mind.

He remembered arguing with his dad about Sian. He'd been so relieved, so proud of himself, when his dad had actually listened to him and not sent Sian away.

He could still hear his grandma's sweet voice talking about Grandpa. She always chuckled when she recounted how they'd met and how Grandpa had walked right up to her and said, "Let's dance, honey".

He missed them already. Missed them terribly. How he wished he could go back and save them all. How he wished he'd conceded the tennis match ten minutes earlier and gone home soon enough to save them. How he wished... anything. He wished anything.

He wished a goddamn genie would come out of the faucet and grant him three wishes. In order they would be: save his family, know who betrayed them, kill them all. One, two, three. Easy peasy pie.

Alder King paced his balcony, feeling both a sense of unease and irritation. He'd sent eighteen of his men to bring in Gavin Ellis, and they had yet to return. Which meant they weren't going to return.

He hadn't thought Gavin would give him any trouble. After all, of the Ellis family line Gavin was the carefree playboy not the stone-cold politician or the unrelenting police chief. Both of whom had been fairly easy to kill. He'd expected to lose men, but over forty to one damn branch of the Ellis family tree was ridiculous.

And now he needed Gavin alive because the rest of the Ellises had gone underground. He couldn't return to London until he'd killed them all. And he needed to return to London. Why anyone would choose to live in a place like this he didn't understand. It was positively uncivilized.

There had to be a way to bring Gavin in without losing any more of his men. He was going to be in enough trouble as it was; he didn't want to return home with a fraction of the army he'd been sent with.

He walked inside and stared at the piles of journals and newspaper articles his men had brought him from Edward Ellis's house. It was time to start reading.

Volume 12; Entry 313; **Jack Ellis***:*

Henry killed his first deer today. He is an apt pupil, and I could not be more proud. His hunter's instinct is strong; his hand steady; his mind pure. He allowed no distractions but focused wholly on the task at hand.

He dressed the deer in mere minutes, using his knife as efficiently as I ever have. I look forward to the day when I can take him with me on a kill. He is so capable and his mind is so strong I do not think it will be long now.

It took a full minute for Sian to remember what had happened when she woke. But then she did, and she wished she hadn't woken at all.

She swallowed a sob, forcing the memories away, and stared across the room at Gavin. He was still fast asleep, face relaxed, worries and tensions of the previous day gone. She wished he didn't have to wake up. She wished he didn't have to face today either. She wished neither of them did.

His eyes popped open, and Sian grinned at him. He grinned back, then he remembered too, and the brightness faded from his eyes, replaced by a hardness Sian hated.

"Time for plan b," he said as he rolled out of his bed.

"What's plan b?"

"I'll let you know when I figure it out."

She almost laughed, but she knew he wasn't being funny.

"We better move on," he said. "I don't want to stay in one place too long." She nodded and started stuffing things into bags. "We'll grab coffee on the way out," he said, voice muffled by the bathroom door. "They have a breakfast. Maybe it'll be more than cereal."

Suddenly she was back in their kitchen, standing over a dead man with milk on his face. Only twenty-four hours ago Owen had been sitting at the kitchen table eating his Crunchy-O's cereal. Then he'd killed several assassins, then they'd killed him. She'd never eat cereal again. Not ever. She wouldn't be able to look at it without seeing that dead man's face and Owen's glassy eyes.

"No cereal," she mumbled, hating that she'd never again hear Owen's stupid way of slurping all the milk out of the bowl.

Gavin touched her shoulder, face tight with grief. "No cereal," he agreed, knowing what she was thinking just like he so often did.

Sian picked up the newspaper outside their door and opened it, gasping at the headline. "Ellis Family under Attack?" She grabbed the wall to hold herself up as she read the first paragraph.

"It's not just us," she whispered. "Uncle Danny's dead. Joseph is dead. Joseph's entire family is dead," she whispered, barely able to believe it. "All of them. Even Laney and Philip." She choked their names out, horrified by it all. Who would kill children? Why was someone killing them? What had the Ellises done?

"I'm sorry," Gavin breathed. "I tried to warn them all. As soon as I knew I warned them. I was too late."

"It's not your fault," Sian said, wrapping her arms around him and hugging him tightly. "It's not your fault."

"I'm the head of the family now. Everything is my fault."

That wasn't true. It wasn't true, but she could see just from looking at him he wouldn't listen to her. The Ellis family was dying around them, and he would bear each death as a mark on his soul. It wasn't fair.

"Tell me what's going on!" she demanded.

"I can't." She opened her mouth to argue, but he cut her off. "I pinky swore."

She closed her mouth and bit her lip. She hated the day they had made the pinky swear pact. She hated that they both felt so compelled to honor it. It was stupid; an agreement between children who didn't know any better. But they were Ellises, and Ellises always kept their word.

Alder took a sip of his tea and grimaced. He missed home. Somehow his housekeeper knew just how to keep a pot of tea hot. There was nothing worse than tepid tea. Unless it was sitting here drinking tepid tea and waiting for news on the runaway Ellises.

He picked up another journal and flipped to a random page.

Volume 15; Entry 17; **Jack Ellis***:*

For the first time Henry has disappointed me. He broke his word. I have explained to him at every opportunity how the Ellises are set apart, and one of the things that sets us apart is that we are men of our word. And women. Bronwen is every bit as capable, reliable, and trustworthy as I am.

But back to Henry. He promised William he would take him fishing this afternoon, but instead he went riding with his friend from town. William sat on the back porch for hours waiting for Henry to return.

I do believe Henry now understands why an Ellis must keep his word. Others depend on us. They expect us to carry through. Otherwise we are nothing. We are no better than anyone else.

The pain of the horsewhipping I gave him should remind him of that should he ever begin to forget.

Alder made a mental note that the Ellises always kept their word, took another sip of his revolting tea, and turned the page.

Sian stared out the window as Gavin drove into the mountains. They were heading towards a cabin a friend of Gavin's owned since they obviously couldn't stay at their own cabin. That would be the first place the killers would look.

It had always seemed strange to her that of all of the Ellises Gavin was the only one who had ever really bonded with the town's people. The Ellises were an integral part of the community, but they were also set apart, above, separate.

She remembered walking downtown with her dad. She remembered the comments she'd heard, the looks she'd seen. "That's Edward Ellis!" people had whispered. They all knew him, but very few approached him, shook his hand, or engaged him in conversation. He was above them, beyond their reach.

It was that way with all the Ellises. Sian and her siblings hadn't attended the local schools; none of the

Ellises did. They were all taught privately by tutors painstakingly chosen by the elder Ellises.

The few times Sian had gone into town and tried to make friends with the local girls she was cautiously tolerated with a mix of hate and awe.

She'd thought once about moving away, about going somewhere where the Ellis name didn't matter, but she couldn't leave Gavin. And Gavin loved Golden. He loved the mountains and the people. He loved it all, and they loved him back. Gavin was the people's Ellis. He was the approachable one, the one with a ready joke and easy smile.

Walking through town with him was a completely different experience than with her dad or Uncle Danny or even Grandma. People waved at Gavin and greeted him with slang. Men slapped him on the back, women gave him their numbers, and all of them grinned when they saw him.

If they only saw him now they would run the other way, Sian thought, watching her brother steer through another curve, hands white on the steering wheel, face tight with concentration.

"Tell me what the problem is," Sian offered. "We'll figure it out together."

He laughed harshly and said, "You're not cut out for this. You don't have the killer instinct."

Irritation flared, but she shoved it down. "Maybe not; but I'm not stupid, and two heads are better than one."

Grandma had always said that. But she'd said it with a wink and usually when they were trying to decide who got to go first or who should get the last piece of cake.

Gavin sighed. "They want me alive."

"Who?"

"The assassins."

"Why?"

"At a guess because I'm the head of the family, and they think I'll know where everyone else is hiding."

"Do you?"

"Maybe; maybe not."

"Why do you keep calling yourself the head of the family?"

"Because I am."

"Why?"

"Damn it, Sian!"

"Fine; keep your secrets," she snarled under her breath. "So what're you thinking?"

"I've never done this!" he snapped, frustration clear in his voice. "I thought it would be easy to grab a guy and make him talk. I hadn't expected them to be willing to kill themselves. Who does that?"

"We would," Sian said softly.

"What?"

"We would. You would kill yourself in a heartbeat if you thought you'd accidentally betray me."

"What're you saying?"

"I don't know. I'm just saying, between you and me, between most of the Ellises, we would happily die to protect each other."

He was quiet for a long time. Finally he said, "So who among us wouldn't?"

Chapter Five

Volume 24; Entry 12; **Jack Ellis***:*

Father is dead. I briefly considered returning to London to visit his grave in order to offer his spirit my apologies and regrets but decided against it. Although my brother was probably overjoyed when I left, I think it best to remain Jack Ellis.

I sometimes dream of those darkened streets, the smell of mincemeat pie hanging in the air. I accept an invitation and move down a side street to be alone. She touches my chest, and my knife tears across her throat, cutting her so deeply she doesn't even have time to scream. I can still feel her warm blood on my hands. A wasted life, draining out onto the cobblestones.

I wonder how those first kills marked me more than later ones. Why I carry them with me, dream of their soft sighs of death, watch their eyes shift to empty? I sometimes dream of completing my task, killing the woman who would become my lovely wife, leaving her dead on the filthy street, and returning to my father's house. I am welcomed, as always.

But when I wake I regret none of my decisions. Father was wrong. I am right. He was blinded by contempt and disgust, but my eyes are open. I see where the true corruption lies. I see filth in every echelon, every niche of society, and I eliminate it when I see fit.

"Who among us wouldn't what?" Sian asked, feeling sick to her stomach.

"Which of us," Gavin said slowly, "of the Ellises, wouldn't die to protect the others?"

Faces swam in her mind, so many faces. Twice a year, every year, the entire Ellis family got together and spent an entire week together. There were a few odd cousins who didn't come, but everyone else was there, in full Ellis style. And Sian loved them all to varying degrees.

Uncle Danny was her favorite uncle. She swallowed a sob. He had been. He was dead. Just like Dad and Mom and Owen and Alice and Grandma. Her cousin Joseph was dead too. And his wife, his children.

"Louise!" she gasped.

"Louise? I don't see it."

"No! I mean, do you think she's okay? I called her, but she freaked me out, and I hung up."

"When did you call her?" he demanded.

"After you left yesterday."

"Sian..."

"Hey, you only made me pinky swear not to leave. You didn't say anything about calling anyone!"

"It was implied," he ground out. "Did you call anyone else?"

"No."

"What did you tell her?"

"Nothing. I asked her what was going on, and she didn't answer. All she would say was 'where are you'. I got scared and hung up."

"I called everyone and warned them," Gavin said. "Even Louise. She'll have known what to do."

"How?! How will she have known what to do?"

"Just will."

She wanted to hit him over the head with a brick. How could she help him if he kept hiding things from her?

"So which one?" he prodded, turning the car onto a bumpy driveway.

"Which one... oh right. Which Ellis would turn on the others? I don't know. It's too loud for me to think." He cast her a slanted look, and she huffed, "Look I need peace and quiet, then I'll think about it. I honestly can't think in this car."

"Sorry, Sian. I know I'm asking a lot."

"You're asking everything," Sian muttered. "And giving nothing."

He parked the car, jogged up the walkway, and pulled a key out from under the dinky firewood box on the porch. "Here you go," he said, handing the key to her. "I need to make some calls. I'll be in soon."

She shrugged, took the key, and walked into the empty cabin. She'd never been angry at Gavin before. Not for real or for long. He was her best friend. Best friends didn't lie to each other. They didn't keep secrets. They didn't ask each other to make a list of everyone in the family that might want to kill them. It made her feel sick inside. All of this was making her feel sick.

But she couldn't let him down. And she'd said she would do it, so she would. She would do it for him. She would do it, but she wouldn't like it.

She found a paper pad and pencil and started drawing a family tree, starting with her great-great-great grandpa Jack Ellis. He had been the first of them. There was absolutely no record of the Ellis line before he'd emigrated from England in 1889.

His eldest son, Henry Ellis, was the head of Sian's line. His second son, William Ellis, had moved to

California when he was sixteen and never returned. Jack's third son, James Ellis, had moved to Denver, but James's line remained tightly entwined with the main Ellis line. Jack's daughter, Mary Ellis, had married into a family of lawyers, and her direct line attended every single Ellis function. There had been a few mentions of other Jack Ellis children, but Sian didn't know their names or where they had ended up.

Thinking of all the Ellises made Sian's head ache. She couldn't help but wonder if any more of them were lying dead somewhere or how one of them could possibly want to harm the others and why.

When she had finally completed her extensive family tree, she carefully crossed out all the names of those she knew of who had already died, either from old age or recent murder. That left her with just over ninety options. She then drew a line through all the children under thirteen, which left her with seventy-two Ellises.

She paced in front of the fireplace, thinking. It made sense that someone might want to kill her dad and Uncle Danny and Joseph. They were all heavily involved in politics and community leadership. Maybe they had crossed the wrong person somewhere along the line. But why Alice and Owen? Why Laney and Philip? Why Grandma?

And why send so many men after her brother? Gavin, the people's Ellis, the friendly one. And how had he killed them all? Like it was nothing!

She felt like screaming, like throwing chairs through the windows. She wanted to beat Gavin until he answered all her questions, until he explained to her exactly what was going on. But she knew he wouldn't. He'd never break a pinky swear. Not ever. And neither would she.

She swiped away a tear. What she wanted most of all was her family back. She wanted to feel her mom's strong arms around her. She wanted to ruffle Owen's red hair. She wanted to run wildly down a hill with Alice, drink nettle tea with Grandma, listen to her dad expound on why corruption among government officials filtered down to the common people. She wanted to play a game of chess with Uncle Danny. She wanted to tickle Laney and Philip until they screamed with laughter.

But she couldn't. Not ever again. Because they were dead. Someone had killed them. And that someone needed to pay.

She sat down with her family tree and started thinking, remembering, carefully plotting, analyzing, and evaluating.

*Volume 8; Entry 79; **Jack Ellis**:*

One of my informants sent me a note today. It seems the governor has developed a taste for beating his wife. My father would think nothing of it. A man has a right to treat his wife as he sees fit I imagine him saying. In fact I'm sure he said that to me at least once.

What a fool he was. Without Bronwen I am weak. I am listless, lost. With Bronwen I am strong, capable, and I know precisely where I am going. A man who treats his wife like chattel is not only a fool but also a corruption to all those around him.

Find the sickness; cut it out.

A miner who beats his wife will affect the lives of his children but very little else. He is a waste of potential, and if he happens to cross my path I will happily remove him, but I will not seek him out.

A governor or a prominent business man who beats his wife is an infectious sore. His very presence will infect all those around him. If the governor can beat his wife, so can I. And I. And I. Why stop there? I will beat my children and my servants as well! Who will stop me? I'm too prominent, too needed. Everyone will look the other way.

Not I. I will stop you.

Gavin felt a distinct sense of helplessness as he dialed Ricky, his last contact. So far no one had anything. How could no one have anything? Even professionals usually left a trail of some kind, even if it was minute.

"I've got something," Ricky said as soon as he picked up.

"Really? What is it?" Gavin held his breath, hoping Ricky's information would be useful.

"So I've got a cousin, Simon..."

"I don't care how you got the info," Gavin interrupted. "Just tell me what it is."

"Fine. Anyway. There's that big house outside of town. The one that Texan built several years ago."

"Yes," Gavin ground out. He hated that house. It shouldn't be there, but unfortunately the previous code enforcement officer had been easily swayed by large amounts of money.

"Anyway, Simon said it's been rented out to a group of foreigners. They don't go down into town, but Simon's made several deliveries out there, and he said they give him the creeps."

"Are they English?" Gavin asked, feeling a frisson of excitement.

"I don't know for sure, but he said they sounded like James Bond."

Gavin grinned. He had them now. They shouldn't have set up camp in his turf. That had been an amateur move.

"Did he get any kind of count?"

"Nah. He just wanted to get the hell outta there."

"Thanks, Ricky; let me know if you hear anything else."

"Sure thing."

Gavin hung up the phone and stared down towards the city for a moment. He'd have to move fast. He knew that they knew that he knew they were after him. So logically they'd be on the move pretty soon. Or at least set up a trap.

He wished his family was with him. He'd be a lot surer of himself if Owen, Alice, and his mom and dad were here. He'd be a lot more confident of his win. But all he had was Sian. He'd have to find a way to use her because it would be madness to go in alone.

Keeping her in the dark was making him feel sick, but he couldn't tell her, he couldn't. He'd never betray his father's trust like that. But in a way he was betraying Sian's trust. If only... But there was no way out of it.

He stared at the cabin door, wishing he could do it without her. He didn't want to open the door and face her again. Her grief and sadness was overwhelming, and it made it harder to push his aside.

He closed his eyes, trying to block the look on her face when she'd read that Uncle Danny had been killed. He'd already found out the day before when he'd called all his contacts, and he'd nearly thrown up.

That was when he'd realized they were going after the entire Ellis family, not just Gavin's line. Someone wanted them all. Someone wanted to kill all the Ellises.

He set his shoulders. He couldn't be weak. Sian was all he had, but she was all he needed. Two Ellises were worth a hundred men, even if they were professionals.

*Volume 2; Entry 289; **Edward Ellis**:*

Silvia and I spoke at length about Sian today. Silvia was ecstatic the day Sian was born. "One of each," she said happily. Now we have two of each. A good balance.

However, I am not certain Sian is capable of the Ellis lifestyle. She excels at the games and is quite capable in many ways, however her tolerance of violence and blood is very small.

Owen got a cut on his head yesterday, and although Sian managed to bandage it, by the time she was finished she was pale and shaky. This is not the first time; she has often shown a distaste for blood. Not at all a good trait for an Ellis.

Silvia reminded me that Sian still has a couple years to mature before I must decide whether or not she can be included. I do not imagine such a severe dislike will change with time, but for Silvia's sake I will give Sian more time.

Alder closed Edward Ellis's journal with a smile. He'd found his angle, his way in, the weak link. Sian Ellis. He'd known she was Edward Ellis's daughter, but he had dismissed her as somewhat inconsequential since she was a woman. She was an Ellis, so she still had to die, but she hadn't been at the top of his list.

But now that he suspected she'd been excluded, it was very likely she would be willing to turn the Ellises over once she learned what monsters they really were. And being a woman she would be incredibly easy to manipulate. They always were.

He tapped his fingers thoughtfully on the side table. She was probably with Gavin which presented a slight problem but certainly not an insurmountable one. How to draw her out?

"Someone here to see you, sir," one of his men said from outside the door.

"Come in," Alder commanded.

One of the locals, wide-eyed with terror, shuffled into the room. "I did what you said to. I told my cousin Ricky 'bout my deliveries. I did what you said, now will you let my family go?"

Alder watched the man sweat. It was pathetic to become so attached to another human being. Ultimately it was everyone's source of weakness. The one person they would do anything for.

"No," Alder said, shaking his head. "I don't think so. Now get out of here, and make sure you keep your mouth shut. Your wife's fairly pretty, and my men are bored."

What little color remained in the man's face completely disappeared. "Please," he begged. "I'll do whatever you ask me to! I'll do anything! Just let them go!"

"You just don't get how this works," Alder said, standing and trailing his fingers over the back of his chair. "As long as I have your family, you have incentive to do as I say. The second I release them... well, where's the incentive? Now get out!"

The man rushed from the room, breath ragged and harsh. "I love the lower orders," Alder chuckled. "Make sure to keep an eye on him," he ordered his guard. "I wouldn't want him to do anything foolish."

"Yes, sir."

Alder stared out the large bay window. His trap had been baited and set. Maybe he wouldn't need Sian after all; he would just wait and see.

Sian jumped when Gavin opened the door. She'd been working feverishly ever since he'd left, and she didn't like what she'd done.

"What're you working on?" Gavin asked, looking over her shoulder.

"I've narrowed it down to seven."

He was silent for a moment as he looked over her disfigured family tree. He traced their crossed out line with his index finger. "It's just us," he muttered."

Sian stared at all the x's with eyes blurry from tears. They shouldn't be dead. Their time, their hour, hadn't truly come.

"Anyway," she said, shaking her head. "Narrowed it down to seven."

"How?" he asked, disbelief clear in his voice.

"I'm not sure, but I did."

"Why Uncle Frank?" he asked, pointing to one of her circles.

She closed her eyes and thought for a moment. "Okay, so Uncle Frank has missed at least six of our bi-annual get-togethers, which on its own may not seem strange, but there's more."

She'd never really sat on the outside and looked at her family. Really looked, and now that she had she was frightened. They weren't normal. Normal families didn't teach their children pharmacology and how to utilize poisonous plants. They didn't teach them code breaking and ancient Greek. They didn't play games like jail break, escape artist, and guard the queen. She didn't actually know what normal families did, but she knew her family didn't do it, whatever it was.

"More what?" Gavin asked.

She sighed, hating that she had to do this. "Uncle Frank wanted to get a divorce several years ago. I heard him and Dad arguing about it one time. Dad said something along the lines of 'you know the rules'. And Frank responded, 'It's the damn 21st century, Edward! Get with the times!'"

She closed her eyes again, trying to remember every word, every detail. "Dad said, 'Ellises don't change with the times, and if you think they do Grandfather made a mistake'. I lost track of the conversation for a second; someone came down the hall and I had to hide. But then Frank said something like, 'Why can't I just kill her?', and Dad replied, 'You're on thin ice, Frank; she's your wife. She's a full Ellis. Let it go.'"

She remembered the look of pure rage on Frank's face when he'd stormed out of the den. He'd left right away and hadn't come to any of the events that year.

"Ever since then he's been different," she said. "I mean, he was always kind of a jerk, but he's been angry. Furious really. I don't think it's reaching to say he'd have an ax to grind with Dad. I'm not exactly sure how Uncle Danny and Joseph come in... but..."

"Don't worry about it," Gavin said. "Just keep going. Who else?"

She didn't want to keep going. "You can read the names."

"But I haven't seen what you've seen."

"I don't want to."

He gently lifted her chin. "You can do this."

"Fine. In order of likelihood, we have Nick, Susan, Alistair, Kelly, Samuel, and Louise."

"Louise?"

"Louise."

"Why?"

She hated this. Really, really hated it. "Don't you want me to start with Nick?"

"No; tell me why you think Louise."

It felt like a betrayal. She loved Louise. She loved them all, but Louise was and always had been her favorite cousin. Sian had felt terrible even circling Louise's name, but she had to be honest. She'd rip her own toenails off later as punishment.

"Last year, Louise met with Dad," she finally said. "When she left she was crying and upset. She wouldn't talk to me for a week. When she finally did, I found out she'd broken up with her boyfriend. They were super serious. She had told me she wanted to marry him, and she wouldn't tell me why they had split up."

"He's a nice guy," Sian said. "I ran into him a couple weeks later, and he looked like hell. He said 'hi' but wouldn't talk to me at all."

"So?" Gavin asked.

"This is so dumb. You know more than I do! I don't even know why you're asking me!"

"Come on, Sian. I need you."

"Fine. I've run through everything in my head, over and over and over. The only thing I can figure is just like Frank, Louise came to Dad asking his permission to marry Noah, and, for whatever reason, Dad said no."

She shook her head in frustration. "What I don't understand is why! Why did they have to get Dad's permission in the first place? Who does that? What the hell kind of family is this?"

"It's our family," Gavin said, gripping her shoulder. "It's ours. What else?"

Sian blinked the tears from her eyes and kept talking. "Louise has been different ever since. Withdrawn, melancholy, just really unhappy. So although I don't think it's likely, I feel she needs to be included on the list."

"Keep going."

Sian swallowed the bile that tried to claw up her throat. "So Nick..."

Chapter Six

Volume 37; Entry 251; **Jack Ellis***:*

My wife is dead. For years she stood by my side and supported me. For years she made my house a home, made my life happier and gentler. She balanced me. I trusted her more than any man. She was more capable than any man. She was everything to me, and I will miss her dearly.

It was my intended exile of John that pushed her to her breaking point. It mattered not to her that John could not carry the Ellis name. She loved him, in spite of his weaknesses.

I explained to her that to keep him near would put us all in mortal danger, but she did not care. She said to me that my legacy was more than what I have so carefully built, more than what I have tended and nurtured and made great. "Every one of your children is part of your legacy whether you wish to include them or not."

For once I could not see it. I could not be swayed to her point of view, nor she to mine. She told me if John left she would go with him. I could not allow that.

It grieved me greatly to kill her. I did it as kindly as I could, slipping a large dose of opium in her evening tea and waiting until she was fast asleep. Then I covered her beautiful face with a pillow and stole the life from her lungs.

John was much distressed by his mother's passing. It made it considerably easier for him to leave us.

Gavin and Sian studied the large, garish house and its grounds from a small rise in the distance. "I count at least thirty," Gavin said, handing the binoculars to Sian.

She tried to focus and count, but her concentration kept slipping. She still felt ill from their conversation earlier. It had taken her over an hour to explain why all seven of her choices might have a grudge against the Ellis line, or at least her dad, the head of the Ellis line.

Which still didn't explain why they had killed Danny and Joseph. It was almost as if someone was trying to wipe them all out. But that didn't make sense.

Examining every one like that had made her question her entire life. Memories of events she'd paid little attention to at the time became prominent, pushing their way forward and demanding her attention.

There was the special camping trip Louise, and all the other cousins close to Sian's age had gone on one year with Sian's dad, Uncle Danny, and Gavin. Sian had been supposed to go too, but at the last minute her mom had gotten sick and asked Sian to stay with her. Her dad had promised he'd take her later that year, but he hadn't.

She remembered thinking that Louise and the others had seemed a little different afterwards. A little more reserved. A little less animated. Gavin was the same as always, but it hadn't been his first camping trip. His first camping trip had been several years earlier with Nick and Joseph.

"So what do you think?" Gavin asked.

Sian jerked. She'd forgotten what she was supposed to be doing. She was supposed to be helping Gavin, not thinking about the past. She quickly scanned the grounds, counting. "Thirty-five. There're five in the greenhouse."

Gavin took the binoculars and looked through them. "Sure enough," he chuckled. "I think you're more Ellis than we ever gave you credit for."

"What?"

"Nothing. So here's my plan."

She listened carefully, and when Gavin was done she said flatly. "That is a stupid-ass plan."

"Yeah, but do you think it'll work?"

"Maybe. Assuming Aine, the goddess of luck, sits on our shoulders the entire time."

He laughed, and she smiled at him. It made her feel rotten that she was glad it had been him to survive. If she'd had to pick, not that she would have, but if she had, she would have picked him. Not because she didn't love the others. She did. She loved them so much it hurt. Losing them left a cavernous hole inside her. But without Gavin she'd be lost.

"So, shall we do this?" he asked.

"No. I don't see her yet."

"See who?"

"Aine."

He laughed again. "She's there. Right behind your ear."

Sian rolled her eyes. "Well in that case, let's get on with it."

She checked both the pistols Gavin had given her, made sure a bullet was in the chamber of each, let the hammers down softly, and holstered them. She hooked all three maces to her pants and slipped the knife back onto her belt.

She felt like she was going into battle, and she was. These men were responsible for killing her family. Now she and Gavin would kill them.

She had never imagined herself killing anyone. She wouldn't have thought she could. But it turned out it wasn't that hard. All she had to do was remember Owen's dead eyes, her mother's slit throat, and Alice's bloody face. All she had to do was remember the desolate look in Gavin's eyes. She could kill these men. She would kill them.

They headed across the ridge to the north side of the hill. It was covered in low brush, and if they were very careful no one would see them coming.

Sian crept low to the ground, feeling like she was playing a game of find the runner. When they'd played against the cousins, she and Gavin had always won just like when they played eliminate the dictator. They won because they were the perfect team. He had the ideas, and she had the marksmanship.

Maybe it would be easier if she imagined they were playing find the runner now. Except instead of paintballs or air softs, her bullets were deadly. And instead of pretend, it was real. She could die. Gavin could die.

She swallowed her fear and kept moving forward, right behind Gavin. He was insane if he thought they could sneak up on and kill thirty-five men. But at least they would die together.

Gavin pushed apart a bush and stepped carefully through. By the time they reached the house it would be sundown, the nowhere time. A good time to launch an attack if the other person doesn't know you're coming. Uncle Danny had taught him that.

Uncle Danny's dead, he thought bleakly. He couldn't imagine Uncle Danny dead. He was so robust. So energetic. So vital. The Ellis table would be dimmer without him. It couldn't be Louise, he thought as he scrambled over a rock. She couldn't have betrayed her own dad, could she have?

He shook his head in disgust. He didn't know anything anymore. All the things he'd been taught, the rules, the Ellises did this, the Ellises didn't do that, were being called into question because one of the Ellises had. One of the Ellises had broken a pinky swear. It made him furious and ill all at once.

Sian's list had been surprising to him. She'd noticed things he definitely hadn't. But she didn't know everything. He'd silently eliminated two of her choices and added three more.

It horrified him that he could actually mistrust eight family members. Mistrust was a disease within a family; it couldn't be allowed. Jack Ellis had said trust was the most important aspect of any relationship; it even superseded love and affection.

He trusted Sian; he always had. If it wasn't for the fact that he'd sworn not to, he would have told her everything right away, years ago, the second he knew the truth.

He tried to pull his focus back to the job at hand. This wasn't the time for reminiscing. Sian was right; his plan sucked. But if he killed them all right here, that would end at least part of it.

He motioned for her to stop. They were right outside the gigantic rock fence, but it wasn't quite time. He wanted to wait until the sun slid behind the mountains to scale the fence and mount his assault.

Alder tapped his fingers together, trying to decide exactly how to play his cards. Just like the weak delivery man, most people had a weakness. A person they loved above all else. And after reading all of Edward's journals, he knew exactly who Gavin's weakness was. But it wasn't simple. The Ellises couldn't possibly be simple.

Alder wasn't sure Gavin would give up his entire family just to save his sister. It was difficult to calculate or measure the love equation. In the end it often turned out that the one someone loved the most was themselves.

He'd once met a man who'd said "you never can tell about yourself", but Alder didn't believe that. He knew himself quite well. He would do whatever it took to protect his own neck, and he would do very little to protect anyone else's.

He'd always considered it essential to know himself. That way he could change what he didn't like and nurture what he did. But that didn't particularly help him with Gavin Ellis.

The way he saw it he'd get the Ellises one way or another. Either Sian would give them to him or Gavin would give them to him. But he wasn't sure which one he should gamble on. It was hard to make educated guesses about people he'd never met. He pulled one of Jack's journals from the pile. There had to be a way to turn the table in his favor.

"Now," Gavin whispered.

All Sian's blood rushed to her stomach, overwhelming her. "I can't do this," she hissed.

"You can. Come on."

He grabbed a jutting stone and started climbing, leaving Sian no choice but to follow him. She reached up, grasping a rough stone and pulled herself after him. Her heart pounded madly. This was insane. They were climbing a wall so they could kill everyone on the other side. It was not like a game of find the runner at all because they could die. They could literally die.

It only took a minute for her to scale the wall, but that minute was long enough to fill Sian with pure dread. They had seen the house and grounds from above, but what if it was different now? What if all thirty-five men were waiting for them right on the other side? What if there were fifty men or a hundred?

Gavin peeked over the top, then whispered, "All clear."

Sian felt a wave of relief, followed immediately by fear. If they weren't by the wall, where were they? Were they hiding around the corner of the house?

Gavin dropped to the ground, and Sian followed him, swallowing a grunt as she landed on the hard ground. Gavin had already pulled his gun, so Sian pulled hers, fingers trembling, heart quaking.

"Stay behind me," he ordered.

She followed him up to the house, then slunk slowly around the side with him, swallowing a gasp when she saw an armed man standing near the house with his back to them. Would they shoot him? And wouldn't that alert everyone that they were here? Her heart was pounding so hard she didn't understand how the man didn't hear it.

Gavin motioned for her to be still and slipped a wire from his pocket. Sian watched him in confusion as he softly crept up behind the man

With lightning speed Gavin wrapped the wire around the man's throat and pulled him backwards. Sian watched in horror as the man struggled for a few seconds, then dropped, nearly pulling Gavin to the ground with him.

Gavin removed his wire, motioned for Sian to follow him, and kept moving. Sian blinked away tears. That wasn't the first time he'd done that. It couldn't have been. He'd been too efficient, too controlled, too cold-blooded.

She blinked her eyes furiously, trying to remind herself why they were doing this. These men had murdered her family. These men would kill more. They would kill Louise. They would kill Nick and his family. They would kill Gavin. She had to do this. If she didn't more Ellises would die.

Gavin snuck up on five other men as Sian watched helplessly. Each time he garroted them quickly and quietly, then dragged their bodies into the shadow of the house before moving forward once more.

He peeked around a corner, then turned back to her. "Time for guns," he whispered. "Stay right beside me. Okay?"

She nodded. Her mouth was so dry she wasn't sure she could speak. This was it. She was going to kill someone. Again. The gun in her hand felt like it weighed a hundred pounds. She swallowed a lump, trying to shake off her fear. She could do this. She had told Gavin she could. She had to do it. It was the only way to protect her family.

Gavin fired around the corner, and the world suddenly exploded. A bullet slammed into the corner of the house, spraying Sian's face with sand. Sian dropped to the ground, forgetting her gun, forgetting that she was supposed to help Gavin, and slapped her hands over her ears. All she could think was she didn't want to die. Not here, not like this.

Gavin moved around the corner, leaving her behind. She wanted to call out for him, she wanted to run after him, but she just couldn't move. She was terrified.

A hand suddenly covered her mouth, and she was ripped to her feet and dragged backwards. In her absolute terror her training deserted her. She knew there was a way to escape the hold, but her mind was too blank to remember.

Instead she dropped out her feet, bit the hand holding her, and fumbled for her mace all at once. Just as she found one of her maces, she was pulled into a small building and the hands released her.

"Please, just listen to me," a cultured voice said softly.

Sian turned carefully, surprised to see a thin, well-dressed man standing behind her, hands empty and held palms out towards her.

"You're Sian Ellis," he said simply.

Sian stepped backward, finger depressing slightly on the mace trigger.

"Please, I don't mean you any harm," he implored. "I won't hurt you. You have my word."

Her breath came hard as she studied his face, trying to read him. She saw nothing. No hate, no anger, no deceit. His eyes were pleading and honest.

"Who are you?" she whispered.

"My name is Alder King. I work for the queen. Your family has committed serious crimes against the crown."

Sian almost laughed. That was surely the most ludicrous thing she'd heard in all her life.

"The queen? As in the queen of England?"

"Yes," Alder said, nodding solemnly.

"Are you for real?" She suddenly realized she had lowered her mace, and she raised it again, pointing it directly at his eyes. She couldn't even trust her family; why would she trust him?

"It's imperative that I locate all the remaining Ellises," he said earnestly.

"So you can kill them?! Like you did my family!"

"I'm so sorry. If there was a way to do this without hurting you, I would. But there are things you don't understand. Things your family has hidden from you."

Sian's hand dropped. Even he knew. A stranger knew more about her family than she did. He knew they were wrong. He knew what crime they had committed. He somehow even knew that she didn't know. That she was less. That she was an Ellis who wasn't an Ellis. She was excluded.

"What do you want from me?" she asked wearily.

"I just want you to read these," Alder said, pulling three leather bound books from the satchel hanging over his shoulder. "After you have, call me." He held the books out to her, a white card on top.

She stared at him, feeling very much like she was making a deal with the devil. She reached for the books, and he put them in her hand. The card lying on top had a phone number written in bold, masculine print. A feeling of dread washed over her, and she suddenly wished she'd never seen him, never touched these books, whatever they were.

When she looked up again he was gone.

Gavin ducked behind a tree and turned to look for Sian. She wasn't there. Panic washed over him. He'd told her to stay right behind him. Where was she?

He leaned around the tree and fired a shot at one of the men running towards him, then bolted back the way he'd come.

"Sian!" he yelled. "Where are you?"

If she'd been killed he'd never forgive himself. He shouldn't have brought her. He should have left her there in the cabin and handled it himself. It's what his dad would have done.

"SIAN!" he screamed, ignoring the gunshots behind him and tearing around the house.

"I'm here!" she yelled, stepping out from a small shed.

"What the hell're you doing?" Gavin yelled, pushing her back inside and slamming the door behind them. They were well and truly trapped now. He pulled her to the back of the shed and started building a barricade out of tools.

"What're you doing?" Sian asked.

"Trying to keep us alive!" he snapped.

"I'm sorry," she whispered. "I panicked. It won't happen again."

Gavin paused. Something was wrong. He didn't hear any gunshots, and there was no one hammering at the door that he'd quickly barred with a shovel.

He dropped the wheelbarrow he'd been putting on its side and walked cautiously to a window. He peeked out. There was no one there.

"What's going on?" Sian asked.

"I don't know."

He'd already killed a dozen men or more, so it made sense that they were cautious in their approach. But he and Sian were penned down in a completely defenseless position, and all the assassins had to do was walk up and shoot the shed to smithereens.

"Let's go," he said, grabbing her hand.

"What do you mean? We're going back out there?!"

"There's no one there."

"What? No. I heard gunshots and screaming."

He heard the fear in her voice and shook his head. He had made a mistake. Affection was making him weak, just like always. His dad had been right. Sian wasn't one of them.

"Let's go," he said again, pushing the door open and walking out into the empty yard. He didn't bother checking. The assassins were gone, and he knew it. Something about this whole thing didn't sit right. He mentally added another name to his list, feeling sick as he did.

Alder grinned as his guard drove quickly down the hill and into the town. He didn't believe in luck; he believed in taking advantage of opportunity when it knocked.

When he'd looked out the window and seen two reddish blonds sneaking around the back of the house he'd known immediately they were Gavin and Sian Ellis. He'd already given his men orders to take Gavin alive, but he imagined they were going to have some trouble with that.

Alder had briefly considered snatching Sian and using her against Gavin, but he wasn't convinced that was best play. He watched them for a moment, trying to make up his mind, but when Sian collapsed to the ground in fear the moment the gunfire began, he knew he had his in.

After the stories his men had told him, he'd expected all of the Ellis women to be a little more hardened and vicious, but Sian Ellis was a true woman. Weak and pathetic. Petrified by the littlest bit of conflict.

When he'd mentioned her family hiding things from her, her face had broken. Emotions were every woman's weakness. She would read the journals, she would feel every bit as betrayed as she should, and she would give him the Ellises.

Chapter Seven

Volume 38; Entry 75; **Jack Ellis***:*
I begin to wonder if my decision to exile John was a mistake. Not only did it cost me my sweet Bronwen, but it seems to have had an effect on Henry as well.

His methods have gotten increasingly brutal, completely lacking any refinement. I fear he enjoys the kill too much.

To be frank, I have always enjoyed the kill. Does the hunter not enjoy the hunt? Does the thrill of it not heat his blood? It does the same for me. However, the ultimate purpose of the kill is to remove corruption so that all may flourish.

I think John and Bronwen both had a civilizing effect on Henry that is now missing. His own wife, chosen carefully, is an excellent Ellis, but she is missing many of the soft attributes Bronwen had. There is a hardness to her that instead of balancing Henry encourages his brutality.

I would not be overly concerned, except that Henry will one day lead the Ellises, and I need to be assured he will make wise decisions.

A council member who uses his power for his own gains but does nothing to support the good of the community, and even uses his power to subjugate other members of the community, needs to be removed. People who are forced to do things they do not wish to do will often force their own will on others weaker than themselves in order to regain a sense of control. And so the corruption filters down.

A senator who uses his status to push his own agenda, all the while ignoring the pleas and requests of his constituents, needs to be removed. When other lesser politicians, such as governors and mayors, look to him for guidance and see how he is abusing his position, they see that they too can ignore the desires of their citizens and do as they please. And so the corruption filters down.

A business man who uses his profits and position to crush other businesses under his heel needs to be removed. His sons grow up thinking the only way to gain power is by destroying the competition at any costs. And so the corruption filters down.

When men see their peers using their power and influence for evil and profiting from it, they decide to use those tactics as well. And so the corruption spreads.

A man who passes you on the street and neglects to nod at you has done no wrong. A man who runs a legitimate gambling hall is not a source of corruption. Even a worthless drunk who refuses to participate in life is not a true source of corruption.

The true definition of corruption is someone who uses their power and influence without care, someone who could be a force for good but is instead a force of evil. Someone like my father, who instead of removing corruption within the upper ranks sent his minions after drunken whores and common people.

I must be sure Henry understands the difference.

"I don't understand what happened," Sian said as they walked slowly back up the hillside towards their car.

Gavin just grunted, and Sian went on. "I mean, why didn't they kill us?"

Gavin grunted again. He knew exactly why they hadn't killed him. What he didn't understand was why they hadn't at least tried to capture him.

"Did you see anything when you were in the shed?" he asked.

"No," she replied. Her voice rose a bit at the end, and he knew she was lying. She had seen something; she just wasn't telling him. She'd never been a good liar. That was one of the reasons she'd been left out, but maybe she was a better liar than any of them had realized.

He glanced at her, studying her profile, remembering her screams of anguish as she'd searched the house looking for Alice and Owen. She couldn't have been the one. He didn't believe it of her. He couldn't. So what was she hiding?

Gavin was freaking her out. He was acting strange, even stranger than before. He was flat. Completely flat. His voice lacked any intonation whatsoever. His face was totally blank.

Sian wanted to tell him about Alder. She opened her mouth to do so but nothing came out. Alder knew her family's secret. Alder knew, and perhaps he'd given her the key to figuring it out.

She'd shoved the books into the back of her pants before she'd left the shed, tightening her belt down to hold them in place, and now they felt like fire against her skin, like brimstone.

She was betraying Gavin's trust, and she felt the whole weight of it. It was making her sick, and she felt like she should be asking him to rip off her toenails. Then she reminded herself he hadn't trusted her first.

"I have to run an errand," Gavin said as he pulled up to the cabin and waited for her to get out. "Don't leave, and don't call anyone. Do you understand?"

"Yes. I won't."

He drove off without saying another word, and Sian watched him go with a frown. He was angry at her. It was practically vibrating off him. Either he knew she was hiding something or he was mad because he thought she was a coward.

She hung her head as shame filled her. She was a coward. The minute bullets had started flying she had panicked, dropping to the ground like a hedgehog. She hadn't had his back. And then she'd lied to him. She was a terrible sister. A terrible person.

"Damn it!" she snapped. "I'm not! He's the one lying, the one keeping secrets!"

She had to be angry to do this, to betray him like she was going to. She had to get mad and hold onto it. It was the only way.

She ripped the door open and stomped inside. She went upstairs to the bedroom she'd picked, closed and locked the door, and sat down on the bed.

She pulled the books out and stared at them, scared to open them and see what was inside. What would they reveal? She felt a whisper of doubt. Maybe Gavin wasn't telling her for a good reason. She should trust him; she should wait for him, tell him everything, and give him the books. That's what she should do.

Owen's pale, dead face flashed before her eyes, and she opened the most worn of the three books. She needed to know why Owen had died.

Entry 1; Jan 1ˢᵗ, 1889:

Here begins the journey of Jack Ellis. I have left my homeland and family behind. I have left my name, my legacy, my future, and here, in this new land, this land of unseen opportunities, I will create new.

I chose the name Jack Ellis on landing for two reasons. "Jack" so I might always remember where I came from, and "Ellis" to symbolize the new.

I saw Ellis Island from the ship. It isn't open to immigrants yet, but it will be soon, and the stories and lives that will pass through it will be unimaginable.

I see no reason to change Bronwen's name. She is not known to anyone, and her name is lovely. It fits her quite nicely. I am already well pleased with her as my wife. She has more sense and insight than any man I have ever known.

I have already spoken to several powerful men in New York, and I have decided to head West. Things are already tightly established here, and I fear it would be harder to build the legacy I desire.

Sian's heart pounded. She was holding Jack Ellis's journal. The patriarch of her family. She'd heard so many stories about him. Her dad had always said how Jack had made Golden the town it was today. He'd said it with great pride, and he'd always reminded them that they represented Jack's legacy.

She hadn't known there were journals. She frowned, wondering how had Alder gotten them. Then she remembered the hidden room. Why would her father have needed to hide Jack's journal? Shouldn't it have been something they all could have read and enjoyed? Obviously not.

She kept reading, entry after entry, and each paragraph she read made her feel sicker and sicker. Jack was not who she thought he was. Jack was... He was... something else. Someone else.

Entry 115:

I killed my first American today. Somehow I thought it would be different, fresher, more invigorating, more memorable. And in some ways it was.

I considered my father's policies at length on the boat ride over the Atlantic, and I discovered the fatal flaw in his reasoning. He claims to seek an end of corruptness, but he begins at the bottom. I can see that corruptness filters down not up. If one wishes to clean something, one must begin at the top.

I chose my prey for three reasons. One, he leered at my wife, an insult I simply could not let pass. Two, his house staff was full of pretty, young Irish women. I could see the despair in their eyes, and I pitied them. Three, he hides behind the facade of a legitimate business man, but in fact he runs several factories manned almost entirely by children. The sight makes me sick.

Bronwen was pleased to help me. She lured the fool into his library where I quickly dispatched him by bludgeoning him over the head with his pretentious Shakespearean bust. I am not so foolish as to leave the blame on his poor staff, so I staged a very convincing break in and stole his most valuable items.

It was rather invigorating, especially with my wife at my side. There was a satisfaction that came with it, a fullness that I certainly never felt in Whitechapel. There is a different sort of energy that comes from killing someone powerful enough in society that his death will actually affect the current of events. Much different than killing a sad, defenseless whore that no one will miss.

Sian dropped the journal like a burning hot coal. Jack. Jack. Jack. Jack Ellis. Emigrant from England. Jack. Jack. Jack. Whitechapel. Whores. Murder.

Their study of history had been very thorough as children. Much of the time had been spent on England and London in particular. In fact, their tutor had spent an entire month expounding on the exploits of Jack the Ripper. In Whitechapel. In 1888.

She rushed to the bathroom, making it with just enough time to vomit in the toilet. There wasn't much in her stomach, so before long she was just dry heaving.

She finally managed to force the heaves to stop and slid to the floor, feeling the cool tile against her face. Jack. Jack. Jack. Jack the Ripper. Her great-great-great-grandfather was Jack the effing Ripper.

Chapter Eight

Volume 5; Entry 182; **Jack Ellis**:

Bronwen took Henry out into the garden today, and I watched them in secret from the upper window. I have almost no memories of my own mother, except the occasional "Keep doing well in your studies, Son" and pat on the head.

Watching Bronwen play with Henry brought up emotions I did not even know I possessed. My father would frown on such behavior. "Play and games belong to the common folk," he would mutter, while going out the door to meet his fellow lords for brandy.

I do not regret leaving. Not for a second. If I ever did, the laughter that echoed up from the garden pathways eradicated it.

I would rather die a poor, unknown man than expose Bronwen and Henry to my family.

Alder tossed Jack Ellis's journal behind him with a sneer. What a fool Jack had been. Certainly he had carved out a small niche for himself in this forsaken land, but it was nothing compared to the power and legacy he left behind him in England.

Jack might have been able to occasionally feed his hunger to kill here or there, but in England he could have killed to his heart's content, moving the strings of the officials like the puppets they were.

It all came back to that worthless concept of love. "Just a tool to keep the common folk in line," Alder muttered, repeating words he'd often been told by his father and grandfather.

But Jack hadn't been common, and he'd still fallen into its trap. With a whore no less. A whore he'd been sent to kill.

Alder shook his head in disgust and stared sightlessly out the window. It was good to know the Ellises were so weak. If Sian didn't work out, he knew just what to do next.

Jack the Ripper. Jack the Ripper. Jack the Ripper. It just kept repeating over and over and over again in Sian's head. She couldn't get it to stop.

How could she not have known? Shouldn't it have been obvious? Shouldn't "descendants of a murderer" have been stamped on each of their heads at birth?

She heaved again realizing that her dad must have known all along. He'd known who Jack was, and he'd insisted they learn all about him.

Their tutor had described each of Jack's London murders in depth, and Sian had had nightmares for weeks afterwards. She was still leery of alleys at night, and she'd had to force herself to follow Gavin the night he'd tried to capture one of the assassins.

Her father had known. Uncle Danny had known. Grandma, Mom, Owen, Alice, Gavin, Louise, Nick. They all knew. But she didn't. She hadn't been told. Why? Was it because of her nightmares? Was it because she'd told their tutor that he could surely think of a more edifying history lesson? Was it because she'd called Jack the Ripper a filthy murderer?

Jack Ellis. Jack the Ripper. He'd married. He'd had children and grandchildren and great-great-great grandchildren. She swallowed a heave and pushed herself up, trying to think past her revulsion and terror.

She splashed cool water on her face and stared into her terrified eyes in the mirror. She shouldn't have taken the books. It would have been better not to know. Because now... Now everything was wrong. The legacy Jack had built, the family that carried on his name, the statue of him in the middle of Washington Street. It was all wrong, tainted, covered in blood, in murder, in lies.

"But it still doesn't make sense," she whispered, trying to figure it all out. She knew what crimes Jack had committed, but why did that matter now? Surely Alder wasn't attempting to exterminate her entire family line because of some women Jack Ellis had murdered over a hundred years ago. It wasn't logical.

She ran through it again in her mind. Jack Ellis, her great-great-great grandfather, was Jack the Ripper. He'd killed people in England, then come to the United States. And he hadn't stop killing. He'd just emigrated.

He hadn't hidden his murderous tendencies from his wife. In fact, she had joined him. They'd killed that man together. So did that mean...?

The other journals. The new ones. She scrambled out of the bathroom and back to her room, closing the door and locking it, hoping Gavin didn't come back for hours.

She picked up both journals, then opened the one with a "1" embossed on the cover in old English script. She gasped, recognizing her dad's strong handwriting immediately.

Entry 1: Grandfather died today. I am now head of the entire Ellis clan. I always knew this day would come, yet

I was still not prepared for the weight I feel upon my shoulders.

Grandfather was a wise leader and a great man. He always knew which path to take, which corruption to remove, which family member to include. I fear I will not be so wise.

I wish my own father was still alive to take up the mantel. I am the youngest Ellis leader, and I'm afraid I will have to be twice as hard.

Sian stared at her father's strong handwriting in confusion. He'd referred to himself as "the head" of the Ellis family just like Gavin had. What did that mean? It clearly gave him some sort of power over all the other Ellises. But she'd already surmised that. The question was why?

She kept reading.

Entry 17: I selected my first kill today. I struggled greatly over whether or not she was corrupt enough to remove. Silvia came to my aid, and we discussed it in length. I finally decided to move forward, and I assigned the job to Danny.

He did not argue as I expected him to. In fact he seemed pleased with my decision. I felt a moment of terror after he left, wondering if I'd made the right call, but then I remembered Grandfather's wise council. "It is better to remove the seed of corruption before it flourishes. If you are ever in doubt, imagine all the seeds that spawn from a single flower head. That is how much corruption one seed will bring."

Although we miss Grandfather's leadership we continue our service to Golden and other areas. There are children who will sleep easier tonight, knowing that their corrupt case worker will not hamper their lives anymore.

Sian stared at the page, trying to understand everything she'd just read. But she could only really understand one thing. Her mother was in on it. Her mother was a murderer. Maybe she hadn't done the killing herself, but she had supported it, condoned it.

She wished she could stop reading, but she couldn't.

Entry 269: Gavin entered the fold this past week, along with Joseph and Nick. I expect great things from each of them. Gavin's bend towards levity concerns me, but Silvia says it will balance the hardness of the Ellis nature. I bow to her wisdom on this. She has certainly balanced me with her encouraging words and gentle touch.

I chose an easy kill for Gavin, a man Gavin already knew to be corrupt. He suffered no nerves that I could tell, not like me and my own first kill, but he has always been the hardest of my children to read.

If Sian had had anything left in her stomach, she would have vomited again. Instead she buried her face in her pillow and cried, remembering that day now, remembering the pale face and quietness of her brother after he'd returned home in the middle of the night.

He'd knocked softly on her door, waking her. She'd let him in, and they had sat in her window seat, backs against the window frame, feet touching. He hadn't spoke, just stared out the window, tears slipping silently down his cheeks. She hadn't asked what was wrong; even then she had somehow known he wouldn't tell her.

She'd fallen asleep at some point, and when she had woken, hc was gone, and in the excitement of the day, she had forgotten. It wasn't every day your older brother turned sixteen. He passed his driver's test with flying colors and took Owen and her out for ice cream. She'd gotten bubblegum flavor because she still thought pink was the coolest color.

She hadn't remembered his pale, tear-stained cheeks in the dark of the night, and she had never thought of it again. She hadn't known that her father had turned Gavin into a killer. How could she have?

She wiped her tears away and kept reading. She read to the end of the first journal, then shoved it away and picked up the other one. It had a "5" embossed on the cover. She flipped to a random page, wishing she could just throw all three journals into a fire.

Entry 89: I have made my final decision regarding Sian. She may bear the Ellis name, but she will never be one of us. She is too soft-natured, too generous of heart, too affected by violence and blood. Beyond that, she is simply too inquisitive, and she wants to know the why of everything.

I understand better now the pain Grandfather felt when he decided Allen was not fit. At the time, I could only agree with him. As much as I loved Allen, I knew he would never be an asset.

It is an entirely different feeling when it is your own child. I've encouraged Sian to expand her horizons, to find something of interest to her. With time I will find her a new place in life and gently push her out.

Sian blinked rapidly to clear the tears from her eyes. Her whole body felt cold and numb. The journal clunked as it fell to the floor, but she made no move to pick it up. She couldn't read anymore. Didn't want to know any more.

She had been measured, and she had been found wanting. It didn't surprise her, not really. What did surprise her was that her own father had been going to kick her out of the family, HAD practically kicked her out of the family.

She hadn't been wanted. He hadn't wanted her. The Ellises hadn't wanted her. But if he hadn't wanted her, why was she still here?

Why hadn't he sent her away like he'd said he was going to? Why was she standing on the outside looking in? Why was she the only one who didn't know? The only one who hadn't been initiated, who hadn't been accepted? Why?

She was so confused. Wasn't it a good thing they had excluded her? Shouldn't she be happy they hadn't accepted her?

She could see it now. She could finally connect all the dots to make a full picture. Everyone in her family was a murderer. They disguised it under the guise of community, of removing corruption, but it didn't matter what they called it. You could dress a pig up, but it was still a damn pig.

Everything made so much more sense now. Why Uncle Frank couldn't divorce his wife. Why Louise couldn't marry Noah. Why sometimes cousins just left and never came back. It explained why Sian always felt a bit lonely at family events. It explained why the adults always had a guarded look in their eyes when they talked to her. It explained why Alice had had a gun, and why Gavin was so good at killing people.

They were murderers. A whole family of murderers. Someone SHOULD wipe them out. They were a blight on society. A self-incorporated judge, jury, and executioner.

"Sian?" Gavin's voice echoed up the stairs. "Are you here?"

Sian's eyes widened and her breath caught in her throat. She couldn't face Gavin now. Not knowing what she knew. No wonder he hadn't trusted her.

"Oh my god," she whispered, suddenly realizing Gavin was the new head of the family. He would be the one to lay down the rules, to tell them who they could and couldn't marry, to tell them who to exile, to tell them who to kill.

She pinched herself hard enough to draw blood. This couldn't be real. It simply couldn't be real. She'd probably eaten bad sushi, fallen asleep reading a terrible novel, and she was dreaming. It had to be a dream. It just couldn't be real. Not her family. Not Gavin. Not any of them.

"Sian!" He was knocking on her door now, an edge of panic in his voice.

She tried to answer him, tried to say "here I am", but she couldn't. He was a cold-blooded murderer. He killed people who didn't live up to the Ellis level of expectations, the Ellis level of correctness, the Ellis level of right.

She screamed as the door suddenly flung inward, ripping the door jamb from the wall.

"Sian!" Gavin gasped, eyes wide. "Why didn't you answer me?"

He stepped towards her, and Sian stepped back. "What's wrong?" he demanded, then his eyes darted down and saw their dad's journal lying forgotten on the floor.

"I can explain," he said.

Sian stepped back again. No one could explain. No one.

"Please; just sit. I'll tell you everything. Please," he pleaded.

She shook her head. She couldn't trust him now, couldn't believe a word he said. He'd been lying to her for years, so many years.

She tightened her hand around Alder's card, feeling its hard edges cut into her palm. "You lied to me," she whispered.

"No!" he exclaimed, eyes full of pain, real or pretend she didn't know. "I never lied to you! You have to believe me!"

"I don't," she whispered, spraying his eyes with her mace and running past him towards the door.

Chapter Nine

*Volume 40; Entry 5; **Jack Ellis**:*
My sweet Bronwen, my wife, my lover, my companion,
my friend. How I miss you. I regret nothing in my life
except losing you. It was selfish of me to try to keep you. I
should have let you go. In the end I kept you in the only
way I knew how.

Gavin stumbled awkwardly down the stairs, gasping
for air and resisting the futile urge to wipe his eyes and
face. He knew from the time Nick had maced him during
training that it was better not to.

He could have stopped her. He could have stopped her
from macing him, from leaving, from running out the
door. But in that split second when he saw her hand move
and knew what she was going to do, he thought maybe it
was better if she left. Maybe it was better if she ran far
away, leaving the Ellises behind her, and started a new
life. A life without them. Without him.

He should have never tried to keep her. It wasn't the
Ellis way.

He gagged as he walked unsteadily to the refrigerator.
He pulled it open blindly and felt around for the bottle of
milk he'd bought earlier. His chest was on fire and his
entire face was burning like he'd dipped it in acid.

He popped the top off the milk and poured it on his face, feeling acute relief as it soothed his burning skin. He ripped off his shirt, grabbed a dishcloth, and scrubbed himself down, then poured the rest of the milk over his head.

He leaned against the counter, breathing shallowly. It would be awhile before he could breathe normally again. He blinked blearily, looking towards the door. She'd left it hanging open on her way out.

He grinned slightly. He was proud of her. She'd actually attacked him. It hurt that she hadn't trusted him enough to listen; but he was glad she had spunk. She knew what he was capable of, and she'd still stood against him. She could have been the best of them.

He wished she hadn't found out that way, but he was glad she finally knew. It helped ease the guilt that had been eating at him for nearly fifteen years. He had no idea what exactly she'd read in the journals, but it didn't really matter; none of it could have been good.

He'd never read them. Only the head of the line was allowed access to the journals, and up until yesterday or the day before, he couldn't actually remember, he hadn't been the head of the line.

He watched the milk drip from his hair into the sink. It made pale circles as it swirled down the drain, and it reminded him of Owen's spilled bowl of cereal.

God he missed them. The idea that he would never see them again still didn't make sense in his mind. Part of him thought if he just drove back out to the house, it would be whole and they would be there waiting for him.

But he knew they weren't. The house was an empty shell. Their bodies had been hauled away in generic plastic bags, and Nick had unzipped them, examined each of them, and written down their cause of death.

For a second he was there, in that cold, white, sterile room, leaning over Nick's shoulder, watching him work, feeling his pain. Nick would have done it. As an Ellis it was his duty, but Gavin knew he would have hated every second.

Just like Gavin hated being the head of the family. He'd known that one day he would accept the mantle of leadership and he would rule as his father had taught him to, but he hadn't expected it to be so soon. He'd expected to have another decade or two to pretend to be free.

He'd never wanted to be the head of the family, but Ellises didn't exactly get to choose what they wanted from life. They were told. And if you were an Ellis in truth, there was only one way to leave the family.

He wiped the milk off his face and walked upstairs to find another shirt. The burning had lessened enough that he thought he could drive now. Of course, if Sian was smart she would have taken the car. He glanced out the window. She had. He grinned. She'd always been the smart one.

Sian drove recklessly down the mountain, dashing tears from her eyes. They'd lied to her. All of them. Dad, Mom, Owen, Alice, Grandma, Uncle Danny, Louise, and Gavin. Her entire family had been lying to her for years, and it hurt. She felt like someone had ripped her heart out of her chest and was using it to play tennis.

She still didn't understand why they had lied, why they had excluded her. She had read what her dad had said about her, and she knew she didn't handle blood and killing defenseless animals very well, but surely there could have been a place for her. Surely they hadn't had to exclude her.

It felt like some sort of cruel joke. She knew she should be relieved they had excluded her from their kill club, but she wasn't. She was angry. She was confused. She was wounded. And she didn't know how to make the pain stop.

She careened around a corner, ignoring the honks of the car she nearly hit, and kept driving. She'd drive far away. She'd drive to California or Oregon or Canada. Gavin had given her a wallet filled with new identification, credit cards, and money earlier. She hadn't questioned him, hadn't wanted to, but she'd thought at the time it was rather strange he just happened to have a new identity ready for her.

Now she didn't think it strange. The Ellises were planners, and they left nothing to chance. If she wanted she could drive for days, and wherever she stopped she could leave Sian Ellis behind and become Suzy Roberts.

She gagged a little at the thought. Suzy Roberts sounded ditzy and boring. Suzy Roberts sounded like the kind of girl who needed men to take care of everything for her. Suzy Roberts sounded like someone who would jump at her own shadow. Sian was none of those things. She hated Suzy Roberts, and she didn't even exist.

She pulled into a gas station and stared at herself in the rearview mirror. She looked like someone who'd lost her entire family, found out they were lying to her, and maced the only person in the world she had left.

What was she doing? She didn't know. She just knew she couldn't go back. Gavin had been lying to her for years. Lying. Keeping her in the dark. Concealing the truth.

She shook her head, disgusted with herself. More importantly, she thought, trying to remind herself, he's been murdering people left and right, because apparently that's what Ellises do.

She wondered exactly how many people the Ellis family had deemed corrupt and executed. And if her dad had been the one to decide who lived and died was it Gavin's job now?

Her head felt like it might explode. It was all just too much, too fast. She stared at Alder's card, lying on the passenger seat. She didn't know everything. She didn't WANT to know everything. She didn't need to call Alder because she didn't want answers. She wanted out.

Alder put his feet up and sipped his aged Scotch slowly. His father would be annoyed that he'd lost another seventeen men to Gavin Ellis, but it had been worth it. He'd seen the look in Sian Ellis's eyes, and he knew she'd break. She wasn't like Gavin. She was a woman. She was weak.

It disgusted him that he even had to bother cleaning up Jack's inferior line. If it were up to him, he'd just leave them to rot. The Ellises would never be any better than they were. Small town fish in a small town pond. No one would ever know they had descended from one of the most prestigious blood lines in England. Their blood was too muddied with common blood.

But none the less, it wouldn't be long until all the Ellises were dead, and then he could leave this hellhole behind him forever.

Volume 19; Entry 152; ***Jack Ellis****:*

I have finally completed the Ellis family canon. It is vastly different from my own family's and much more comprehensive. For instance, my father took little notice of women.

Bronwen has been a wonderful asset to me. Without her steady guidance and help, I am certain I would not have succeeded so well. I have counseled Henry strongly that when he looks for a bride, he must find a woman whose mind and body will be strong enough to bear the Ellis ways.

As for my own children, I have already decided that William cannot be included. Even as a child he showed a tendency towards weakness. I can only think he inherited it from my own father. A family is only as strong as its weakest member. I will not allow my house to be riddled with weakness and feeble mindedness.

I will weed out those unfit to be Ellises, and I will only include those fit to share the Ellis name. My family will be stronger and more unified than my father's ever was.

Sian's fingers trembled as she paid for the pre-paid phone with cash. She wanted to walk away. She wanted to leave the Ellises behind her, but she couldn't. Not yet.

She sat in Gavin's car and carefully dialed.

"Hello?"

"Louise, it's Sian."

"Sian! Where are you?"

"No; I'm not going to tell you. I just want to know, was it you?"

"Was what me?"

"Are you the one who betrayed us?"

Sian still wasn't convinced someone had betrayed them. There was a possibility Alder or someone else in the British government had stumbled across something that had revealed the location of Jack Ellis and his descendants. She just didn't know why they would care.

"Betrayed? What do you mean?" Louise asked, voice full of disbelief.

"I don't know. Gavin said someone in the family betrayed us."

"But I don't understand. To who? And why?"

"I don't know! I hoped you would know, seeing how I'm the only Ellis who doesn't know ANYTHING!!!" Anger crept into Sian's voice. She still couldn't believe it. All the pinky swears she and Louise had made, all the whispered secrets over pillows in the dark of night, all the plans of adventure.

"Sian... I can't... The fact is..."

"How many people have you murdered?" Sian demanded.

"I don't murder people," Louise hissed.

"Fine, how many people have you EXECUTED?"

"You don't understand," Louise said. "You couldn't possibly understand."

"I know. That's why I'm out here, in the cold, with no idea what's going on."

"Tell me where you are; I'll come get you."

"You haven't answered my question."

"Which question?"

"Was it you?"

"No; damn it! Why would I do that?! My dad is dead! Just the same as your dad! How could you even think I would betray them?" Louise's voice broke, and she added softly, "I would never."

"Not even for Noah?" Sian whispered, feeling terrible for pushing her.

"Goddammit, Sian! This is my FAMILY! My loyalty is to them!"

"I'm sorry," Sian mumbled. "I just... I'm so confused. How could... Why didn't you ever..." She shook her head and hung up before Louise could respond.

Gavin picked up the discarded journal from the floor. It was one of his father's; he could tell immediately. And he knew it was the page Sian had been reading because it was stained with tears.

He read the entry.

Entry 89: I have made my final decision regarding Sian. She may bear the Ellis name, but she will never be one of us. She is too soft-natured, too generous of heart, too affected by violence and blood. Beyond that, she is simply too inquisitive, and she wants to know the why of everything.

I understand better now the pain Grandfather felt when he decided Allen was not fit. At the time, I could only agree with him. As much as I loved Allen, I knew he would never be an asset.

It is an entirely different feeling when it is your own child. I've encouraged Sian to expand her horizons, to find something of interest to her. With time I will find her a new place in life and gently push her out.

Gavin closed his eyes, still seeing the pain in Sian's eyes, the hurt, the betrayal, then he turned the page and kept reading.

Entry 91: Gavin confronted me about my exclusion of Sian from the camping trip, and I told him my decision. He did not take it well.

I had always considered the closeness between my children to be an asset. It never occurred to me what would happen if I had to send one away.

Sian and Gavin are so close that my exclusion of her affects him greatly. His eyes were desolate when I told him. He insisted that even though Sian doesn't like blood she's just as capable as he is. I really had no argument for that. I agree with him. But I did not tell him the entire truth. Sian's inquisitive nature makes her a liability I cannot afford.

Gavin has never opposed me on anything, but he was quite clear on his position. If Sian leaves, so does he. He knows I cannot allow that. The rule is quite clear. There is only one way for an Ellis to leave. Death.

The easiest solution would be to kill Sian. A neat little car accident would take care of things nicely, and any one of the Ellises would carry out the task if I gave it to them. However, I am uncertain that is the best path to take.

Gavin stared at the journal in disgust. How could his dad even have considered it? Exile was one thing, but to kill Sian just because she didn't have the stomach to be an Ellis?

A wave of nausea rolled over him. He hadn't realized he'd almost gotten Sian killed. It just proved that she was better off without him.

He imagined her somewhere far away, California maybe, where the ocean would buffet the beach. She'd be taking photographs along the tide pools, and she'd meet someone nice. Someone she didn't need permission to marry. He felt a pang of sorrow imagining it, knowing she'd be alone, without family until that imaginary day, but maybe that was better.

He read the entry again. He'd never really thought anything of Sian's inquisitive nature. She asked a lot of questions to be sure, but he didn't understand why that made her dangerous to the Ellises. It's not like his dad hadn't always had the answers.

Everything he'd ever assumed about Sian was called into question. To a degree he'd understood when he'd thought her squeamishness was the reason his dad had excluded her. He'd never been able to imagine her killing anyone because she gagged at the little bit of blood.

But she had killed someone, several someones, when she'd been in the alley with him. But then she'd fallen apart at the house and hidden in the little shed. Not that he blamed her. It had been his first gunfight too, and frankly, it had been a little terrifying. He'd only kept going because he knew it needed done.

Gavin shook his thoughts away and kept reading. He wanted to know why his dad hadn't ordered her killed after all.

I recall Jack's words about Henry. How John had balanced Henry and that perhaps sending John away had been a mistake.

Gavin will one day be the head of our family. I think he has great potential to lead, but not if he is stripped of all humanity.

If Sian remains in the dark perhaps her presence can yet be beneficial.

He frowned, irritated at his father's phrasing, but he kept reading, trying to see exactly WHY his dad had decided to leave her he

Entry 105: I have told the others of my decision. There was some protest, especially from Frank, but overall, my ruling was met with acceptance.

There may still come a day when I have no choice but to remove Sian. Someday she might want to marry and have children, and I cannot allow the Ellis family to be infiltrated with weakness. I will tolerate her for as long as it benefits Gavin, but once her usefulness is over, I will do what I must.

Pure fury filled Gavin. He'd always known that each of them was akin to a chess piece, being moved around at will, but he couldn't stomach the blatant use.

He was suddenly glad his dad was dead. Glad he'd been shot in the chest so many times his heart had been torn to pieces.

He forced himself not to tear the journal to shreds and breathed deeply. He couldn't allow his judgement to be clouded by emotions. He was the head of the Ellis family now. And just like his father, he had to consider the wellbeing of all the Ellises. He couldn't just protect Sian. He had to protect them all.

It was his fault really. Not his dad's. His dad had only been trying to take care of everyone. It shouldn't have surprised Gavin at all that his dad had been willing to kill Sian to protect the larger family.

There were a set of rules. His dad had bent them to include Sian, but if Gavin hadn't opposed him in the first place, she would have never been in danger. She would have been free of the Ellises years ago and happy.

It didn't matter if Gavin was happy, and he shouldn't have tried to hold on to the one thing that made his life bearable. He should have let her go a long time ago. She needed to be free.

For a minute he allowed himself to imagine her drinking wine at an art opening, laughing at something a handsome stranger said, having children that were free of the Ellis ways.

Then he pushed thoughts of her away and started to plan. There was corruptness inside the Ellis family, and he needed to find it.

Chapter Ten

Volume 5; Entry 28; **Jack Ellis***:*
I sometimes find myself wondering what Father would think if he were here with me. Would he be able to see the truth of my path? The rightness? Or would he continue to be blinded by his supposed superiority?

I've composed a dozen letters to him over the last several years, asking his forgiveness, his understanding, his blessing, but I always burn them. I do not need him to tell me I am doing right. I know that I am.

Since my arrival the town has started to clean up nicely, and every kill proves the truth of my argument. Remove a corrupt sheriff, and lawlessness dissipates. Remove a corrupt business man, and everyone prospers. Remove a corrupt preacher, and the flock becomes more faithful, more true.

I have made a difference. I have changed the world for the better. Some men would argue that my methods are wrong, but I have never met two people with the same definition of wrong, and if it is so easily changeable, then there is no TRUE right or wrong.

Alder glanced impatiently at his watch. Sian was late. Which meant he was going to have to sit in this filthy den longer than necessary. He'd have to remember to make her pay for that.

He watched with a sneer as a child sitting in the booth across from his shoved a chip in its mouth. He hoped it choked.

Children were not meant to be seen or heard. He'd seen his own children once a year until they were eighteen. Then he'd married the girls off and sent the boys to train with the Elites. They had never eaten in his presence. That was strictly for the lower orders.

Sian walked slowly into the restaurant, scanning the crowd, looking for men in pressed shirts and pants. This had been a mistake, agreeing to meet Alder, but she wanted to know what he had to say and how exactly he thought he could justify killing the Ellises.

She felt hopelessly exposed, and she wished she hadn't left the guns and knife Gavin had given her back at the cabin. She found some comfort in the weight of the three maces swinging from her belt loops, but she would have preferred to have a gun and a full clip.

She'd never used maces before, and she wasn't sure if the one she'd used on Gavin would still work. She glanced around anxiously. Surely Alder wouldn't try to hurt her here, in such a public, crowded place.

Her neck tingled, and she turned. He was waiting for her in a small booth with four of his men in the booths on either side of him. They stuck out in the crowded restaurant like cigars in a domino box.

He made a small gesture for her to come over, and she paused. She didn't trust him. His face seemed sincere, but there was something about the lines around his eyes and lips that bothered her. She just didn't know why.

She could still run. She could run and never look back. She could build a new life, under a new name. She could leave it all behind, leave Gavin behind.

She swallowed her fear, walked steadily through the crowded room, and sat across from Alder.

"Did you read the journals?" he asked, fingers templed below his chin.

"Not all of them," she admitted.

"But enough?"

"Not really. I still don't understand what this has to do with you or England or the queen."

"You don't?" he raised an eyebrow and made a tsking noise like she was a stupid child. "Then I shall explain."

Sian glared at him, disliking the way he looked at her, like she wasn't good enough somehow. Her family could reject her if they wanted, but Alder King didn't know anything about her, and she'd be damned if she'd let him make her feel like she wasn't smart enough or good enough.

"Jack Ellis was a murderer," Alder said slowly, over-enunciating "murderer". "He murdered over twenty people in London before coming to America."

"I thought it was only five," Sian said, feeling a perverse need to argue.

He shrugged a slim shoulder. "Five that were attributed to him through the newspapers. The details of the other fifteen were not released to the press."

He was lying. She knew he was lying because if Jack had killed more than five their tutor would have mentioned it. Their father would have made sure of it.

Alder waved the waitress away and continued. "He was considered number one on the list, if you understand what I mean, but once he stepped foot in America, all trace of him was lost."

"What was his real name?" Sian asked.

Alder ignored her question and kept talking. "Occasionally word would reach England of a murder done in a similar fashion, but no one we sent was ever able to find him."

Sian eyes narrowed. His story didn't make any sense. "Once he left," she said, "why did anyone even bother looking for him? He was gone. No longer your problem, right?"

He smiled gently, like she couldn't possibly understand and said, "We take our duty very seriously. Surely you can understand that."

She did understand duty, but she still didn't believe him. She was starting to feel very much like a deer that had walked right into a trap. She glanced behind her, wondering if she could make it to the door and out into the parking lot before them. This whole thing was making her antsy.

She jerked when he slipped his hand over her own. "All I ask is that you listen, Sian. I'm telling you the truth. Has anyone ever told you the truth?"

Tears filled her eyes. She couldn't even trust her own family. She couldn't even trust her best friend. How could she trust him? How could she trust anyone? He squeezed her hand gently, and some of his warmth passed into her cold fingers. She wished she could give it back to him; she hated the feel of it.

"Anyway," he continued, leaving his hand on hers. "As luck would have it, one of our computer technicians recently discovered an article featuring the Ellis family and all the good they've done for the Golden community.

A photograph of Jack accompanied the article, and it was easy to piece the puzzle together from there."

Sian felt a rush of relief. No one in their family had betrayed them. Just Aine, the goddess of luck. Probably because Ellises didn't believe in luck.

"I still don't understand!" she exclaimed. "Jack is dead. Why were you still looking for him? And why kill his family? Jack may have committed those crimes, but no one in my family has ever even been to England. Not once. Why are you here? And what right do you think you have to kill them?"

"Don't you see?" he asked, eyes burning with intent. "Jack Ellis was our responsibility. It was our job to find him and to see justice served. Our failure to do so gave birth to an army of conscienceless murderers."

Sian flinched at his words. It may be true, but she didn't like hearing it. Lying or not, murderers or not, they were still her family.

"It is our job," Alder said emphatically, "our task, our charge to deliver justice long overdue."

"Even the children?" she whispered. "They haven't done anything wrong."

"We have been charged with killing the entire Ellis line; however, after meeting you I see doing that would not be true justice. So I have decided that going forward we will only kill the initiated members."

He smiled comfortingly as he said it, but Sian felt uneasy. There was just something about him she didn't trust. On the other hand she'd trusted her own family for twenty-four years and they hadn't been worthy of it, so maybe she wasn't the best judge of character.

"What do you want from me?" she asked, needing to know why he'd approached her in the first place.

"Gavin," he said simply.

She blinked, covering the hate and rage that filled her. "Just Gavin?" she asked.

"Just Gavin," he agreed, smiling like he'd already won.

If she still had her gun she would shoot him where he sat, but she hadn't come prepared. Because she wasn't a true Ellis.

"Why Gavin?" she asked. "Why me? And what do I get out of it?"

Irritation flashed in his eyes, but he smiled and said, "Gavin because he is the head of the Ellis family. We need him to find the others."

She'd figured that.

"You because you are the only Ellis who has not bathed in blood. You understand that they must be stopped. They are murderers. They are a bane to society, and you are the only one who can possibly see that. You do see that, don't you?"

She didn't. She knew they were murderers, but she wasn't sure about the bane to society. The Ellises had done a lot of good. In spite of their obvious failings, they protected the little people, which was more than most prominent families did.

"They betrayed you," Alder said, eyes hard. "They lied to you day in and day out. They looked at you and saw nothing."

It was true. And it hurt. But she was an Ellis, through and through; and there was no way in hell she was going to sit here one more minute with Alder King, the man who wanted to kill them all.

She threw her water cup in his face, jumped to her feet, and ran swiftly towards the door.

"They betrayed you, Sian!" Alder yelled behind her.

She ignored him, crashed through the door, and sprinted towards her car. Alder didn't understand the Ellises at all if he thought she would give up Gavin or any of the others. She would never. Not ever. She'd sooner die.

She fumbled for her car keys but was jerked to a stop when someone grabbed her from behind. Her jiu jitsu training immediately kicked in, and she dropped to the ground, escaping her attacker's hold, and swung her foot around, sweeping him to the ground.

She grabbed one of the maces and sprayed the other four men barreling towards her, then pushed to her feet and ran. She could hear more right behind her, but she was light on her feet and she sprinted as hard as she could towards downtown.

She didn't know Lakewood as well as she knew Golden, but she did know that as soon as she was around a bunch of storefronts and lots of foot traffic it would be easy to lose them.

She ducked down a side street and ran as fast as she could towards the main shopping street. She skidded onto the sidewalk, glanced quickly behind her, and kept running. There were five men chasing her, but they hadn't turned onto the street yet. This was her chance.

She pushed into a crowded boutique and ran towards the back of the store. She ignored the owner's protest, burst out the back door, and ran down the alley as fast as she could.

She paused to take a breath, looking all around her. She was alone in the alley so she grabbed a fire escape ladder and scrambled to the top of the building. As soon as she was over the ladder and on top of the roof, she dropped down flat.

She knew they wouldn't be able to see her from the ground, so unless they climbed up every escape ladder looking for her, she should be safe.

Her breath came fast and hard. She'd screwed up. She should have never called Alder, should have never listened to him. He was lying every bit as much as her own family.

Gavin's face flashed before her eyes. "I never lied to you!" He'd said it so earnestly, but it couldn't possibly be true. How could he not have lied to her? He'd lived a whole different life without telling her a word.

She closed her eyes and tried to remember. Memory after memory rushed through her mind. Gavin and she exploring the woods together. Gavin and Owen helping her climb on top of an old, crumbling building. Baking cookies with Grandma, Gavin, and Alice. Sitting around the fireplace listening to Dad talk about politics and ways to improve the community. Laughing silently whenever Mom argued with him and told him he was wrong about something.

But Sian remembered Gavin most of all. They'd always been inseparable. Even before she could walk. Their mom used to laugh about how Gavin had carried Sian around in a pack everywhere he went even though he was only four.

Moments flashed through her head like a slide show. Gavin and she skipping rocks. Gavin and she having a tea party; he'd come as a knight and saved her from dragons. Gavin and she going to a drive-in movie. Gavin and she arguing over whether lager was better than ale.

There had been days when Gavin was down and Sian had read him old Gothic novels to cheer him up. There had been days when Gavin had been excited and full of pizazz, and they'd gone out on the town and found some kind of event to be part of. She smiled, remembering the time they'd polka danced at the community center.

There were so many memories it hurt. Happy memories, fun memories, memories full of love. But there had been an undercurrent to everything, an undercurrent she'd never noticed when she'd been living those moments, but now that she was remembering, she could see it.

The Ellis family reunions. The odd aura of power that followed her father around. The times she'd heard one of them come home late at night for no reason. The constant comings and goings of other Ellis family members. The games, the tutors, the classes.

Had she known? Had she always known something was wrong? That they weren't quite right? Maybe she had. She shook her head in frustration. How could she have known? She'd never known anything else. And that still didn't change the fact that Gavin had lied to her. Hadn't he?

When she'd ask him what they'd done on the camping trip she'd missed, he'd replied, "We went hunting."

"Did you catch anything?"

"Couple of small game."

Sian had cringed and let it go at that. But even if Gavin had meant people instead of animals, he hadn't technically lied.

She frowned, remembering something else. Not long after she'd turned sixteen Gavin had stormed angrily out of their father's study. His face had gone white when he'd seen her, and he'd grabbed her hand and pulled her out of the house with him.

"What's wrong?" Sian had asked.

"Nothing. I just had a fight with Dad."

Sian hadn't responded for a moment. Gavin was so easy going he never fought with anyone. Not even Nick when he was being a royal butthead.

Finally she'd said, "What about?"

"You," he mumbled.

"Me? Why?"

"He wants to send you away to boarding school."

Sian stumbled, and Gavin caught her elbow, holding her upright. "What? Why?" Sian gasped. "He hasn't said anything to me."

His eyes had shifted to the side, but he'd said, "He thinks you should broaden your horizons. He talked about Switzerland or France."

"France?!" Sian exclaimed. "But I can barely even speak French!"

Gavin shrugged. "I asked him not to send you. You belong here. With us."

"What did he say?"

"He said he'd think about it."

Boarding school had never come up, and Sian had always assumed her dad had listened to Gavin. She'd never asked her dad about it because she didn't want to go away. The idea of leaving home, of leaving Gavin, had terrified her.

She opened her eyes and stared at the puffy white clouds overhead. Gavin had fought for her when her dad had wanted to send her away. That was why she was still here. Even though she hadn't been an Ellis in truth, Gavin hadn't wanted her to go.

"What the hell have I done?" she whispered, feeling wretched inside. She'd run away from the one person who had never lied to her, and now she was all alone.

*Volume 2; Entry 210; **Henry Ellis**:*

I find I do not enjoy being the head of the Ellis line. Father handled it so efficiently and with such confidence. He was always sure of his path; and he never questioned himself or regretted his decisions.

Except perhaps with John. I was displeased to read of our mother's death, and it called into question everything I know of Father. Was Mother corrupt for wishing to leave? Would it really have exposed our family if she had? I do not know. I think perhaps for once he was not honest.

I sometimes dream of a simple life, far away from politics and control. I dream of apple orchards and milking cows in the morning. I imagine my children and grandchildren laughing in the fields, no longer burdened by death and murder.

But I know it will never be. I am already too deeply embroiled. There is no escape. My children and their children and their children are all part of this. Part of this system Father built, this madness.

Gavin stood outside the rustic meeting house for a while, watching the Ellis family mill around inside, waiting for him. It had taken them over five hours to assemble, but now that they were here it was time for him to take charge.

Sickness rushed up his throat, and he vomited in the bushes. He stood there for a moment, head resting on the wall, hands holding his weight, shudders wracking his body.

He wasn't ready for this. He wasn't strong enough or hard enough or Ellis enough to pull this off. How could his dad have done this to him? How could he not have lived?

A hand settled on his shoulder, and Gavin spun, knife already drawn.

"Settle down, cuz," Nick said softly, taking a step backward. "You okay?"

"No," Gavin gasped, glad it was Nick and not someone else. "I can't do this."

"Sure you can."

"Nick... I... You don't understand. You don't understand what it means to be the head. You don't understand the weight, the responsibility, the..." Gavin swallowed a ball of bile.

"Your whole life has been training for this," Nick said. "You were always the head. Your dad never let you forget it. Not for a minute."

Gavin heard the resentment in Nick's tone and knew it was for him, knew Nick was remembering all the times Gavin had been berated for the slightest errors or the smallest missteps.

"I feel like a goddam kid about to ask lions to balance on stools," Gavin confessed.

Nick laughed and said, "Just imagine the lions in their underwear. Works for me."

Gavin grinned. "So you're with me?"

"You know I am," Nick replied, all trace of levity gone.

Seconds later Gavin stepped from the shadows into the light and faced his entire family. He swallowed his fear and channeled his father, trying to be Edward Ellis.

"As you should all know by now, Edward Ellis, head of the Ellis line is dead," Gavin announced. "By rule, I am now the head."

Frank stepped forward with a snort. "Forget it! I'm not taking orders from a snot-nosed brat!"

Gavin's eyebrow twitched. He'd never liked Frank. No one did; but he was family. "I am the head," Gavin repeated.

"Fat crap. I'm not taking orders from you. Furthermore, you never cared much for the rules or else Sian wouldn't still be here!"

There were a few murmurs of agreement, and Gavin sighed. They were going to force him to take control the difficult way.

"For all we know," Frank continued, "Sian's the reason all this happened!"

"She's not," Gavin said.

"How do you know?"

"I know. What about you?"

"What about me?"

"You had reason to see the head of the family gone. Perhaps you're the one who betrayed us."

Frank laughed. "What makes you think that?"

"An argument you had with my father several years ago."

Frank paled slightly, but Gavin didn't divulge any more details. Instead he turned to the room at large and said, "In fact, there are several here who had motive to destroy the Ellis family. Your corruption will be revealed in due time, but now we have a war to fight."

"I propose we take a vote!" Frank yelled. "Whoever wins becomes the new head."

"This is not a democracy," Gavin declared.

"Well maybe it should be."

The rest of the family was starting to argue now. Gavin needed to end this before he lost control. "You all know the rules," he said evenly. "There is no choice, no vote, no majority rules."

"I think it's time for a change," Frank ground out, moving closer.

Frank's eyes were hard, and Gavin knew he was coming in for the kill. He waited until Frank was only three feet away, then he ripped his garrote out of his belt, wrapped it around his uncle's neck, and squeezed. He ignored the gasps of disbelief from his assembled family, ignored his uncle's clawing hands and bulging eyes, ignored the rush of guilt he felt for killing an Ellis.

When Frank finally stopped struggling, and Gavin was sure he was dead, he released his garrote and dropped Frank's body to the floor.

Gavin lifted his head to face the Ellises, eyes snapping, jaw hard. "I am Gavin Ellis, by right, head of the Ellis family! Does anyone else wish to challenge me?!"

They took a collective step back, and Gavin breathed a small sigh of relief. His father had taught him that the most efficient way to rule was by making an example as quickly as possible. It was just one more thing Gavin wished his father was wrong about.

"These men, these assassins came into our town, into our home, and they've been hunting us like dogs. It's time to stop hiding!" Gavin shouted. "It's time for the Ellises to go to war!

Chapter Eleven

Volume 10; Entry 63; **Edward Ellis***:*
I begin to fear for the future of the Ellis line. When Jack began all those years ago I'm certain he had not considered a future when there would be so many of us. It becomes difficult to handle and control the many branches and members.

Only yesterday Nick requested my permission to move to downtown Denver. I have no need of him in Denver because Frank's family controls the Denver area.

Still I might have considered his request if he wasn't already situated exactly where I need him to be. Nick has never been particularly happy with his position as coroner, but that is where I need him, so that is where he will stay.

There has not been a single Ellis whose request I have not denied at some point or another. Some take it well because they understand and respect the rules, but others do not bow to my rule, or Jack's rules, so easily.

It was a simple matter to say they were going to go to war, but having said it, Gavin wasn't entirely certain how to carry it out. Everyone had arrived prepared. They had their guns, their knives, their batons, their syringes, and their wires. So he had an army, but he wasn't sure where and how to fight the war.

"I want each of you to reach out to your contacts. We need to know where they are," he said, figuring locating the assassins was the first step. "They're English. There're still a large number, at least fifty or more. Someone has to have seen them."

"They're English?" Alistair asked in disbelief.

"Yes; highly trained and extremely committed."

"And you say their goal is to wipe out the Ellis line?" Alistair snorted. "For what reason?"

"I have no idea what their reasoning is," Gavin ground out, trying not to feel like a child arguing with his elders. "I've engaged with them twice, and they didn't try to kill me either time. Which tells me they need me for some reason, and the only reason to need me is to find all of you."

Alistair ran a hand through his silver hair and gave Gavin a condescending smile. "Or perhaps, you made all this up. Perhaps you were tired of being under your father's thumb. Perhaps you killed him, Danny, and Joseph. Perhaps there are no 'villains'."

Gavin growled softly. Maybe his example hadn't been big enough or extreme enough. How many Ellises was he going to have to kill before they accepted his rule?

"Or it could be you," Gavin countered. "Maybe you were sick of watching from the sidelines as my father, Danny, and Joseph controlled all the major fields. Perhaps you thought to eliminate me as well, and then gain control of the family through some sort of democratic vote. Perhaps you and Frank were in on it together," Gavin accused softly.

Alistair paled and stepped backward. "I had nothing to do with your father's death, I swear."

"You have more motive than I do," Gavin said, eyes hard. "I would have always eventually ruled, but you never would have."

Gavin stepped forward into the spot Alistair had just vacated. "If you want to challenge me, do it," he growled. "But stop hiding behind your fancy wordplay."

Alistair glanced behind him and saw that no one was with him. Everyone had backed off, leaving a gap of ten feet or more behind him. Furthermore, all the younger Ellises had moved to stand behind Gavin, showing their full support.

Alistair paled even more and stammered, "I do not wish to challenge you."

"Are you sure?"

"I am sure. You are the head of the Ellis house by right of birth."

"Yes," Gavin said. "Yes, I am. Now I gave an order. Carry it out!"

Several members jumped in surprise, but they all began to separate and pull out their phones. Except Louise. Louise worked her way through the crowd to Gavin.

"Where's Sian?" she demanded.

"I don't know," Gavin said.

"What do you mean you don't know? She's in danger! How could you have left her hanging in the wind?"

Gavin ignored the panic her words made him feel. "She's only in danger if she's with us. She found out, Louise; and she ran."

"I kinda figured."

"How?"

"She called me."

"Again or just once?"

"Again."

Gavin's heart started to pound. It had never occurred to him that she would stick around. He thought she'd hit the highway and just keep driving.

"Where was she? What was she doing?" he demanded.

"That's what I'm asking you."

"I don't know. I thought she'd just drive. I thought she'd go to California or... I don't know, Hawaii."

"How did she find out?" Louise asked.

"She somehow got ahold of some journals."

"Journals? Jack's?" Gavin shrugged. He didn't really want to go into detail. "How?" she demanded.

He hadn't figured that part out yet. The only thing he could figure is that someone at the house had given the journals to her. Someone who had already read them. Someone who knew who she was and that she was Ellis is name only.

He felt the blood slowly drain from his face. Someone who knew how important she was to him. Someone who would use her to get to him.

"Gavin? What's wrong?" Louise was gripping his shoulder and shaking him lightly, but Gavin couldn't respond.

How could he have been so stupid? How could he have let her go? Now he had no way to find her and no way to protect her. He should have never let her go.

*Volume 65; Entry 17; **Jack Ellis**:*

I have begun to long for home. I miss the filthy London streets with vendors crying out on the corners and sweepers waiting to clean a path for me across the street. I miss the ancient, sturdy architecture. I miss the sound of my own people.

I'm sure everything would be much altered if I were to see it now. Sixty-five years is a long time to be away from home. I wonder if my ancestral home still stands. I wonder if my brothers are still alive.

Everything surrounding me grows dim, pale, and small, but the call of London grows stronger every day. I would, just once, like to revisit that dark corner on which I met Bronwen. Would she laugh if she knew it was her smile that saved her from my knife?

I fear old age is making me weak and sentimental. Yesterday I thought I saw Bronwen on the stairway, waiting for me. Would she welcome me? I do not know.

Alder tapped his fingers on his desk in irritation. Sian Ellis had disappointed him. He honestly hadn't expected her to remain loyal to her family once she discovered what they had done. What they were doing. What they were.

Loyalty is nearly as confounding as love, he thought agitatedly as he sipped his tepid tea. Very well. Since Sian wouldn't give him the Ellises he'd just have to implement plan b and hope that love trumped loyalty.

He still needed Sian though. He sighed deeply. He would never understand why women always felt the need to run. He always found them eventually. They were only postponing the inevitable and, quite frankly, irritating him in the process. And when he was irritated he wasn't very nice. Someone needed to pay for his wasted time.

"Bring me the woman and her children," he ordered his guard.

"Yes, sir."

"Do you know why you're here?" Alder asked as his guard shoved the delivery man's wife against the wall.

"No," she stuttered.

She was paler and more cowed than she had been five days ago. Captivity must not agree with her. Alder smiled kindly and said, "Sian Ellis is making me wait. I'm so sick of waiting. I hate it here. I hate the mountains; I hate the people; I hate the word 'beer'. Peasants, all of you."

He rubbed his temples, wondering exactly what it would take to make the throbbing go away. But he knew. Gavin Ellis's head on a platter. All in good time, he thought with a sigh.

"So, while we wait we'll play a game. Which one of the children would you like me to kill first?"

She started sobbing, and both of the children scrambled to hide behind her.

"I think as their mother," Alder continued, feeling better already, "you should be the one to pick." He smiled widely, interested to see how it would all play out, and added, "Of course, if you prefer, I can kill you instead."

Sian lay silently on the rooftop for hours, waiting for night to come. The sooner it came, the sooner she could escape from her own thoughts and the questions that kept cycling through her head, over and over and over.

Why hadn't her dad thought she was good enough? What was it that Alice and Owen and Gavin had that she didn't? What did the entire Ellis family have that she didn't? What was wrong with HER?

As the sun slowly moved across the sky, Sian thought of a thousand reasons why she might have been excluded. She didn't like blood. She couldn't run fast enough. She had missed the bull's eye that one time they'd played eliminate the dictator. She'd failed her eighth grade pharmacology class. She'd thrown up on Uncle Frank one year after she'd drank too much spiked eggnog.

It was mind numbing, and by the time dusk came, Sian felt like she was the worst Ellis who ever lived.

Glad to finally be moving so she could stop thinking so much, she climbed down from the roof and searched the streets warily for overly dressed men. She didn't see anything suspicious, but what did she know? She wasn't an Ellis. She was Suzy Roberts. Just a silly, ditzy blond trying to keep from getting killed.

She walked aimlessly for a minute, cursing her stupidity. She couldn't possible go back to her car; she was certain Alder would have left men to watch it. And she was too scared to call Louise or any of the other Ellises. She was truly alone.

Gavin had destroyed their phones, so she had no idea how to contact him unless she called Louise first, but she'd maced him and run away. Surely he wouldn't want anything to do with her now. She hadn't even given him a chance to explain himself.

She suddenly had an overwhelming urge to go home. Logically she knew it wasn't home anymore. She knew it was burned. She knew her family had died there. She knew a murderer had built it. But it was her home.

She'd dealt with all life's problems there. When she'd failed pharmacology class, Grandma had stayed up with Sian every night in the kitchen, going over the terms and explaining everything time and time again until Sian had finally passed.

When she turned sixteen, Gavin had taught her how to drive by letting her drive up and down the driveway for hours at a time.

She'd sat in the garden and pulled off rose petals to decide whether or not she should date Chet Martin. Then she and her mom had laughed about how many roses Sian had destroyed to get the answer she wanted.

She and Owen had hidden in the tree outside her window the time they'd "accidently" exploded a cake in the kitchen.

Gavin had buried his dog under that same tree.

Sian had kissed Chet Martin and broke up with him the next day under that tree.

It may have been built out of lies, but it was still her home.

Chapter Twelve

Volume 6; Entry 73; **Edward Ellis***:*

It will not be long before I can welcome Owen into our ranks. He shows great promise, and I'm certain he will handle the transition smoothly.

I sometimes wonder if it would not have been better for him to be the eldest. He has a sternness to him and a seriousness that Gavin lacks. I'm not sure Gavin possesses the necessary hardness to keep the Ellises in line.

Gavin has always been jovial and kind. There have been several times when I have had to enforce my rule with unquestionable brutality, and I fear Gavin does not have it in him.

Gavin waited impatiently for someone to report something useful. With as many fingers in as many pies as the Ellises had, it was ridiculous that no one had anything to offer up.

His phone rang, and he answered with a short "What?"

"It's Ricky."

"Yeah?"

"So my cousin, the one who told me about the house on the hill?"

"Get to the point," Gavin snapped.

"They have his family."

Gavin frowned. "What do you mean?"

"They took his family. That's why he told me about them, because they told him to."

Gavin's mind whirled. They had set a trap for him. Interesting. He was beginning to think he hadn't given them enough credit. Their leader was clearly quite clever if he'd thought to use Gavin's own informant system against him. Gavin laughed shortly. He hated being outplayed.

"So why'd he fess up?" Gavin asked. Most people knew better than to cross the Ellises. It may be an unwritten rule, but it was still a rule.

"They took his family with them when they left the house. He doesn't know where they are, and he's hoping you can find them."

Gavin rolled his eyes. "Tell him his family's already dead. That's the price he pays for not coming to me in the first place." The line was silent, and Gavin could only imagine the look on Ricky's face.

"I didn't kill them," Gavin ground out. "I'm just saying. Does he have anything useful to say?"

Ricky's voice wavered when he finally replied. "He said the leader's name is Alder King. He didn't get a solid count, but he thinks there are at least a hundred of them."

Gavin mentally subtracted the seventeen he'd killed, figuring there were between eighty and a hundred men remaining. He glanced out at the Ellises. If he took away the kids and older ones, he had a solid fifty-five. That was probably fair.

"Anything else?" he demanded.

"He was just trying to protect his wife and kids."

"He should've known the only way to do that was to come to me right away. If I had known I would have launched a sneak attack and saved them instead of going into a trap alone and nearly getting killed. If they're dead it's his own fault. Call me immediately if you find out anything else."

"Yes, sir."

Ricky had never called him "sir" before or used that deferential tone of voice. That's how people talked to his father, but his father was dead. Gavin was the new Ellis.

"I've got a lead," Tony, one of Gavin's younger cousins, said.

"What is it?"

"One of my guys saw twelve black SUV's head into Lakewood this morning."

"Alistair!" Gavin shouted.

Alistair looked up from his phone and started walking slowly towards Gavin. Gavin briefly considered killing him just to make a point, but he needed every Ellis he had, and he couldn't afford to keep killing them just because they were unhappy with his rule. Besides he needed Alistair alive because Lakewood was Alistair's turf. If something was happening there Alistair would be the one to find it.

"What?" Alistair finally asked.

"Call the chief of police in Lakewood," Gavin ordered. "We need a lead on twelve black SUV's. The leader's name is Alder King. There're eighty to a hundred of them, and they're English."

"You can't just use the chief of police for personal business," Alistair sputtered.

Gavin laughed dryly. "That's exactly what the Ellises have been doing for nearly a hundred and fifty years. Call him, or I'll replace you."

Alistair paled, nodded shortly, and walked off.

"You figured it out quick enough," Nick said, tone amused. "Did the underwear trick help?"

Gavin swallowed a laugh. "You know, just for a second there when Frank was arguing with me I imagined him wearing a banana hammock."

Nick cringed. "I don't see how that could have possibly helped."

"It didn't. You're on Sian's short list."

"Her short list?"

"Of family members who might be willing to betray us."

"Really?" Nick replied with a chuckle.

"Actually her conclusions were fairly legitimate. She's paid a lot more attention over the years than I think any of us gave her credit for."

"I didn't," Nick said earnestly.

"I never thought you did."

"Where is Sian?"

"I don't know. I let her run away. She actually maced me." Gavin laughed lightly, but then he sobered and said, "I shouldn't have let her go. So much was happening so fast I hadn't put together that someone was using her against me."

Nick gave an exaggerated gasp. "You mean you're not infallible? I thought the head of the Ellis line was always infallible."

"What would you do?" Gavin asked suddenly. "If you weren't an Ellis?"

Nick's brow furrowed. "I don't know."

"Don't bullshit me. I used to lay awake at night dreaming about what I'd do." He'd never been able to figure it out, but that hadn't stopped him from trying.

"So what would you do?" Nick asked.

"I'd be one of those river raft guides," Gavin lied with a grin. "I'd grow my hair out and say things like 'gnarly' and 'rad', run around without a shirt on, and let all the ladies touch my rippling muscles."

Nick laughed loudly, and several Ellises turned to stare at him. Then he said quietly, "I'd move to the Western Slope and start up a vineyard and winery. But it would be one of those ones where we crushed the grapes with our bare feet, you know?"

Gavin closed his eyes for a minute, imagining it. Nick, his pretty blond wife, and their three towheaded brats jumping up and down in a bucket of grapes laughing like mad men.

"And we all fall down," Gavin whispered.

"What?"

"Nothing." He stared out at the Ellises for a second, then asked Nick a question he'd been avoiding. "Did you find anything on the bodies?"

"The assassins or..."

Gavin shook his head. He was doing his best not to think of his family, not to remember their dead bodies and dead eyes. "The assassins," he said quickly.

"No."

"I didn't think you would. Anyway, do me a favor and call the coroner in Lakewood; see if he's heard anything."

"On it."

Gavin watched Nick go with a pang of sadness. He wanted Nick to have that vineyard. He wanted him to squish grapes with his toes. He wanted Sian to run on the beach in California. He wanted the Ellis children never to feel blood on their hands. But that wasn't the Ellis way.

People are so predictable, Alder thought as he buffed his fingernails. He chuckled, remembering the children's terrified howls when their mother had decided the boy should be the one to die first.

If she really loved them, she would have chosen herself. Not that Alder had expected her too, and he'd have been disappointed if she had. Now, if he didn't kill them, her children would grow up knowing she didn't love them at all.

Love. What a ridiculous concept. Just like "duty" and "honor", "loyalty" and "morality". Made up ideas, all of them. The only thing that really mattered in life was power.

But some people, people like Gavin Ellis believed in concepts like love, honor, and duty. Unlike the mother who'd been willing to sacrifice her children to save herself, he was certain Gavin would give up anything for Sian. Maybe even the rest of the Ellises.

Alder's phone rang. He glanced at the ID and sighed, then answered with a short, "Hello, Father."

"Alder, why haven't you called?"

"I have nothing to report."

"What do you mean?"

"Just what I said."

"Why?"

"They've all gone underground, like foxes."

"Well throw fire into their den and get the job done!"

"I have never failed you before, Father," Alder ground out. "I will not fail you now."

"See that you don't!" his father snapped before disconnecting.

Alder resisted the urge to hurl his phone against the wall. He wasn't an idiot; he knew how to hunt. Granted his father had only ever sent him after one person at a time not a whole bloody clan and the Ellises were slightly more skilled than Alder had originally expected. Regardless, he would get the job done, just like he always did; it just wasn't going to be quick or easy.

"Jimmy," he called out.

"Yes, sir?"

"Have you found the girl yet?"

"No, but we will, sir."

"Think like a woman," Alder snapped.

Jimmy paused, clearly unsure what Alder meant. After a moment he carefully asked, "How so, sir?"

"They're creatures of habit. They like comfort. They don't feel safe exposed in the open. Just like a rabbit. They'll try to make it back to their burrow even if that's not the best thing to do."

Alder grinned widely. "In fact, I think I know exactly where to find her."

Chapter Thirteen

Volume 2; Entry 198; ***Jack Ellis****:*

The family rooms are now completed. Bronwen insisted we put the nursery right off the master suite. For a moment I argued with her, explaining that just isn't the way things are done; but then I looked at her with her flashing green eyes and wild red hair, and I knew I would lose the fight.

If she wants to keep Henry close to us, who I am to argue? She has already proven herself a much better mother than my own mother was.

I heard her singing a lullaby to Henry last night as she rocked him to sleep. I couldn't understand the words; she often speaks to Henry in Welsh, but her voice is so beautiful; it filled me with peace.

Sian paid the cab driver and started up the long driveway to her home. She'd spent most of the night in the taxi, driving around town. She'd wanted to go to the house right away, but she hadn't wanted to go at night. She knew it was ridiculous, but she needed to see everything in the light of the sun.

Her heart pounded anxiously with every step. She dreaded seeing it burned and ruined. When she finally topped the driveway she stopped and stared, feeling like she'd walked into a brick wall.

Overall the house looked just the same as always. The stone walls were white and strong. The green tile roof was the same roof Jack had installed when he'd first built it. It looked just like home.

Except it didn't. The master bedroom's balcony hung haphazardly towards the ground, floor boards broken and black. The windows behind the balcony were gone, staring at her like empty eye sockets.

She could still see her mom, standing on the balcony, curly hair blowing in the wind, setting sun turning her face golden. She'd been so beautiful. And now she was dead.

Sian closed her eyes, seeing the house as it was meant to be, whole and strong, just like her family. She saw Alder's smirking eyes; she saw his lying mouth move, and she hated him.

He had taken everything away from her. Her family. Her home. Gavin. Her security. Everything. She clenched her fist, wishing she had been strong enough to kill him, wishing she'd just killed him with a fork in the restaurant and been done with it.

But she hadn't. So she'd have to figure something else out. She walked mechanically towards the side door just like she had a million times before. But this time she knew there was no one there to greet her. She remembered laughing with Gavin that last morning, when she'd thought everyone was still alive. She ignored the police tape and opened the door with fingers numb from distress and fear.

There was still a small, foolish part of her that had hoped it was all a terrible dream, but the blood was still there, no longer vibrant red but a rusty brown. If she hadn't seen it fresh, she might not have even known what it was. Except for the smell. She could still smell it, and it made her stomach roll.

She forced the nausea away and stepped into the entry way, feeling the mirror glass crunch under her feet. She heard the echo of her grandma's voice yell, "Wipe your feet!" from the kitchen.

"Yes, Grandma," she whispered.

Sian wiped her feet automatically, then walked into the kitchen, remembering the smell of shortbread cookies and coffee.

"You want some cookies, Sian darling?" Grandma asked, hugging Sian's shoulders and kissing her hair.

"Yes." Sian sat on a stool and spun around in a circle.

"Stop that," Grandma chided. "You'll make yourself sick."

"Gavin does it."

"And do you remember the time he had to clean up the kitchen floor?"

Sian stopped spinning and watched Grandma slide the hot cookies onto the cooling rack. "Do you miss being a baker?" she asked.

Grandma laughed. "Of course not! I worked from three in the morning to ten at night! Now I only bake when I want to."

A wistful look passed over her face. "The only thing that would make my life better is your grandpa."

Sian dunked her cookie into a glass of milk and shoved it into her mouth.

The memory fell away as Sian stepped over the yellow tape marking the outline of a dead man. Grandma would never bake cookies again. And why? Because Jack Ellis was a madman.

Sian ground her teeth. Jack may have been a madman, but that wasn't why her family had died. Her family had died because of Alder King. He had killed them.

She flinched as dry Crunchy-O's snapped under her feet. Owen would never eat Crunchy-O's ever again. He was dead.

She walked down the hallway in a haze, imagining the screams and yells there must have been. Had they all been in the kitchen to begin with? Why hadn't her mother made it upstairs with the others?

She stared at the outline at the bottom of the stairs. It seemed so crass, so harsh that all that was left of her mom was a dried blood stain and some yellow strips of tape roughly marking where she had died.

Sian knelt beside the tape, running her finger along it. It hurt that they'd kept an entire part of their lives from her. All of them. Every one of them had held her at arm's length, only letting her so close, only letting her be part of a little bit of their lives.

She wiped the tears from her eyes and turned to go up the stairs. Memory took over, and suddenly she was at the top coming down.

"You look amazing!" Gavin said as she stepped slowly down the steps.

Chet Martin was taking her to dinner and a play. It was her first real date, and she was dreading it. Her palms were sweaty; her dress was too tight; she felt sick to her stomach.

"My little girl, all grown up," Dad said as he held out his hand to her.

Sian giggled softly. "I feel silly in this dress."

"You look beautiful."

"My legs can barely move."

"Then you can't run away," Gavin laughed.

"But what if I need to run away?"

"Chet's a good guy," Gavin said seriously. "He'll treat you right, or he'll have me to answer to."

"And me," Owen said.

Sian smiled at them. "With two such scary brothers I guess I don't have anything to fear, huh?"

"Not a thing," Dad said, kissing her on the cheek.

The glow of the memory evaporated. Dad was dead. He'd never yell at her, never kiss her cheek, never sneak her another piece of chocolate cake under the table.

Sian stumbled on one of the steps and caught herself with her hands. The fire hadn't spread this far, but she could smell the acrid char coating everything. She could smell the damp of the water.

She stepped slowly down the hallway remembering a particularly long game of solve the murder they had once played over a rainy weekend. Mom had been murdered in the library with the meat fork. Sian had been the only one to deduce that Grandma had killed her. She should have never complained about the bunt cake being heavy.

She breathed out slowly, trying to block the waves of memory. She shouldn't have come. There were too many memories. A week ago they were happy memories, but today they were sad. Because her family had been stolen from her. It hadn't been their time.

She felt another flash of anger at Jack. Why couldn't he have been a normal great-great-great-grandpa? If he had been normal, her family wouldn't have died. If he had been normal, none of this ever would have happened.

How could someone be so sick? How could he have turned his entire family into murderers? How could her father have made Gavin and Owen and Alice kill people?

How could he have watched on with pride, feeling happy that they had succeeded and would go on to kill many more? She didn't care what reasons they thought they had, what justification, they were still a bunch of murderers.

She suddenly thought of all the other children who'd grown up in her house. All the other children who had been initiated. And the ones, like her, who had been turned away. She passed her bedroom and wondered which of her aunts or uncles had grown up in it. Had they cried themselves to sleep the night they'd first killed? Or had they liked it?

She shuddered, thinking of Alice. Had it been the night of her sixteenth birthday just like Gavin? Who had she killed? How had she done it? Tears poured down her cheeks as she imagined Alice stabbing some random person in a back alley. Sunny, crazy Alice. Sweet, serious Owen. Both with blood on their hands.

"Damn you, Jack," she whispered, stepping closer to the master bedroom he'd once slept in. She wondered how many times he'd walked down this hallway, just as she was. Had he thought about his descendants? Had he wondered what they'd be like?

How many times had he washed blood off his hands in the sink? She'd always been proud of her family's mark on the area. She'd been proud of Ellis buildings and Ellis donations and Ellis grants. She'd been proud of how much they'd influenced Golden. But she'd never known the truth. She'd never been introduced to the dark.

The fire had crept out the door of the master bedroom like gigantic, black spider legs, crawling down the walls of the hallway. She stopped and stared, heart pounding loudly. She didn't want to go in. Her memories had all been happy. But now they were tainted. Tainted with blood.

She turned and went into the nursery. She and Owen had shared the nursery for a while since they'd barely been a year apart.

She had a vague memory of Gavin visiting them. He'd rocked Sian in the rocker after she'd banged her head on the window seat. She remembered the melody of his quiet singing. She couldn't remember the words now, wasn't sure if she'd ever known, but she remembered feeling safe.

The wooden rocking chair was gone now. Burned to the floor with everything else. The pillows that her great-great-great grandma Bronwen had embroidered were gone, burned to ash. Sian had used to tuck them under her head when she had curled up on the window seat to read Pooh Bear.

The blocks they'd played with. The old wooden horse that Henry Ellis had built. The doll with the missing eye. All gone. Burned. Erased by fire, like they had never been.

The wall between the nursery and master bedroom was totally burned out, and she could see the lump of ash that had been her parent's bed. Where her mom had played peek-a-boo with her. Where her dad had tickled all her little toes.

Everything was gone; they were gone. She slipped to the floor and sobbed, missing them more than she would have thought possible. She missed Owen and Alice. She missed Dad, Mom, and Grandma. She missed Gavin. She didn't care that they had lied to her. She didn't care that they had excluded her. They were her family. She loved them. She missed them. She wanted them back.

Volume 4; Entry 8; **Henry Ellis***:*

I have often wondered if Father even thought of us, even once considered the burden he placed upon our shoulders.

I knew from the time I was twelve what he expected from me. I told my own son, Richard, when he was fifteen. I wanted him to have a few more years than I had. I didn't want him to know, didn't want him to look at me with anything less than love and adoration. In spite of my wishes, Richard told Stewart, my eldest grandson, when he was only ten.

All of us, the line of eldest male Ellises, know exactly what is expected of us. What Jack expected of us. What I don't understand is why we keep doing it.

I sometimes feel him and think if I turn I'll see him standing just behind me, ready with a word of praise. But I turn, and he's not there. He's gone, and I find the lack of his wisdom makes me cold. I hate him. I hate him for forcing this upon me.

But truth be told, I miss him terribly. I miss the slight lilt to his words, his cheerful smile, his inquisitive eyes, and his well pondered ideas. I miss his warmth and his praise. If he were still here, I think I could bear all this weight with ease.

"I think I've found them," Nick said, pulling Gavin into a corner.

Finally, Gavin thought. It was nearly morning. With as many informants as the Ellises had he could hardly believe it had taken all night to find anything.

"Where?" he asked.

"Just outside of Lakewood. Another vacation house."

"Let's roll out then," Gavin said with a grin.

"Do you have a plan?"

"Not really. This is a little different than what we normally do."

"You don't say."

Gavin laughed. "I say we go out there, get as close as we can, sneak in, kill everyone." He raised an eyebrow. "Actually, if you think about it, it's not that different than a game of save the hostage. In fact, there may be an actual hostage. A local and her kids."

Gavin shrugged a shoulder and added thoughtfully, "All that sneaking around takes a lot of effort, so maybe we'll just bust the gate in instead. And then kill everyone. Except, of course the hostages."

"I like you as the Ellis head," Nick said with a laugh. "You've got style."

"Not sure Dad would've approved."

"You'll get the job done, just like you always have" Nick said. "That's all that matters."

"Let's do this," Gavin said, hoping Nick was right.

He turned to the group at large. "I think we've located them. I want everyone who hasn't been out on a run in the last year to stay here with the kids. The rest of you come with me."

There were murmurs, and some of the murmurs were dissatisfied. After a tense moment, Susan stepped forward, face anxious, hands twitching nervously. "Should we... don't you think... I mean, I don't mean to challenge you, but why can't we let the police handle this? It's not what we normally do."

"And how would you like to explain it?" Gavin said.

"Explain what?"

"It, this situation, to the police."

Susan blinked a few times, then stepped back, clearly unable to think of a suitable explanation. She'd married in about ten years ago, and it was one of the few times Gavin thought his dad might have made a mistake in judgement. She didn't have the stomach for the Ellises. But once you were in, you couldn't exactly leave.

"Does anyone have anything else to add?" Gavin asked. No one said a word. "Would you like to explain to me, Alistair, why the police chief didn't have any information for us?" Gavin demanded.

Alistair paled and shifted his feet anxiously. "I don't know. Perhaps he just didn't have time to find anything yet."

"It seems strange to me that the Lakewood coroner would have more information than the Lakewood police chief. Doesn't that seem strange to you?"

Alastair shrugged and said, "I didn't go out last year."

So that's the way it was, Gavin thought with irritation. "Everyone who didn't go out in the last year," he clarified, "except Alistair, Susan, Kelly, and Samuel." He didn't bother including Louise or the others he'd added to the list; he already knew they'd gone out in the last year.

Alastair stuttered, "But you said..."

"I changed my mind. It's my prerogative. Now load up."

Gavin headed towards the door, taking Nick and Louise with him. If he was going into a fight he wanted them by his side. Out of the corner of his eye he saw Alistair and Susan conversing in frantic whispers, and he hated that he would kill them both in a heartbeat to keep everything under control.

Chapter Fourteen

Volume 7; Entry 41; **Jack Ellis***:*

I find I very much enjoy being a father. Henry is such a bright child, so quick to learn. Today as I watched him train his dog to fetch I allowed myself to indulge in an imagining of the future.

A future where my sons have sons and daughters of their own. A future where my house is large and powerful, capable of bringing down the most corrupt and influential persons.

It pleases me to think of such a future. It pleases me to think of Henry's children growing up in the same house as he did, learning the same lessons he did, becoming strong and wise as he will.

In a hundred years the Ellis mark will be larger than my father's mark ever was. In two hundred years it will be embossed into the very earth.

Sian blinked frantically, trying to clear her eyes of tears. She'd come here to think, to figure out a plan, not to sob until she couldn't cry anymore. She pushed herself to her feet, rubbed her eyes with the back of her hand, and walked carefully across the burned floor towards the walk-in closet.

She pushed aside the police tape and walked through the sagging door frame. This time she knew there would be no magic on the other side. Just lies.

The yellow outlines were here too, looking overly bright and cheerful on the blackened floor. But otherwise there was not a bit of color in the secret room. Just the absence of color, black.

She couldn't help but wonder if Alice had even been recognizable by the time they got the fire out. She shook that thought from her head and looked around, trying to see if there might still be anything useful, but there wasn't.

She sat on the floor in between all those yellow markings and closed her eyes. The fact that her dad hadn't trusted her made it harder for Sian to trust herself. She'd always felt very self-assured. She'd always thought she could take on anything and win. They had raised her to think that way.

But in the end her father hadn't deemed her worthy, and it made her feel unworthy. It made her feel small and incapable. She'd never felt that way before, and she hated it.

She remembered a pretend trial they'd had once in the Ellis library. She'd played the defense attorney, her father had been the judge, Louise was the prosecutor, and Gavin, Owen, and the remaining cousins were the jury.

Sian had convinced the jury that Nick wasn't guilty of embezzling from his non-profit company, which of course he was. She remembered thinking at the time her father hadn't seemed pleased, but she hadn't known why.

She'd played the game using every tool at her disposal, and she'd won. Wasn't that the point? But she could see now it wasn't. The point was to remove corruption and disease, "to leave the world a better place" as Uncle Danny often said.

They really believed it. They really believed that what they were doing was right. Sian tried to think of all the people they might have killed, but she couldn't. She'd never paid attention to the news or the things going on around her. She'd just lived.

She'd never thought it strange how many members of her family had influential jobs. It had never bothered her that everyone in town treated the Ellises with a strange sort of deferential fear. She'd never wondered why she didn't have any place in the community like everyone else. Gavin was the city planner. Owen was the county clerk. Nick was the coroner. Louise was the city's tax lawyer. Even Alice worked as a journalist for the local newspaper.

"I'm so stupid," she whispered, feeling very alone. It was no wonder her dad hadn't trusted her; she hadn't even been smart enough to see what was going on around her.

But the truth was Sian was an Ellis. She could see that now. She'd been trained like them, she'd been prepared just like them, and she was capable. She knew she was capable.

She also had an uncanny ability to read people, and she knew with certainly Alder King wasn't going to stop until all the Ellises were dead. That included her and all her cousins' children, and, most importantly, Gavin.

She couldn't let that happen. Gavin had always protected her, always. It was time she protected him. She just had to figure out how.

A plan started to form in her head. She would call Alder and tell him she'd had a change of heart. She would make it clear that she would come to him, and then she would kill him.

She frowned wondering how exactly she would do it. It was like a backwards game of jail break. She was deliberately going into jail not breaking out, but she still had to kill the guard with whatever was available at the time.

There was a gigantic safe built into the wall of the library that held all the Ellis family guns, but she didn't know the combination, and she was fairly certain Alder wouldn't let her near him with a gun. She could take one of the knives from the kitchen, but it would be hard to hide and transport since she didn't have a sheath.

She still had her maces, but she was pretty sure she couldn't kill him with mace, and he would probably take them away before she got close enough to try. She needed something she could hide. She wished she had paid more attention to her Aunt Letty's lessons on poisonous plants. There were at least six in the garden, but she didn't know which ones they were.

She tapped her fingers on her knee, trying to work it all out. In addition to guards, Alder would certainly be armed, so a projectile weapon would be better than getting in close. She bit her lip and tried to think of something, anything, that she could sneak in and kill him with, but she couldn't think of a thing.

"That's not acceptable!" she snapped. Alder King was trying to kill her family, and she loved her family, every murderous one of them. So somehow, somehow, she needed to find a way to kill him.

A memory suddenly popped into her mind. She was standing in front of her mirror and her mom was behind her, twisting Sian's hair into a knot.

"A woman's greatest asset," her mom was saying, "is that she is often underestimated."

"Why is that an asset?" Sian had asked, standing on her tippy toes so she could see what her mom was doing better.

"Because, darling, most men won't think you're smart or capable or deadly, and that makes you all the more dangerous. They'll never see it coming."

Sian had frowned, still not understanding, but liking the long, pointy sticks her mom pushed through her hair to hold it in place.

"Just remember, Sian darling, never correct a man if he thinks you're a fool."

"I correct Gavin all the time."

"So you do, my love. So you do."

The memory faded, and Sian jumped to her feet and ran down the hallway to her room. She skidded to a stop just inside and stared. It was totally trashed. Someone, Alder's men probably, had tossed and broken everything.

With a cracked sob, she picked up the broken snow globe by the door. Uncle Danny had given it to her for Christmas one year. He'd said it reminded him of her. There had been a little girl inside pulling a sled, but the little girl was gone now, broken and crushed under careless feet.

Sian twisted the screw and listened to the song play. It sounded terribly loud in the empty house, and it filled her with sadness. She would never hear Uncle Danny's belly laugh again. Not ever. She hated Alder King. Hated him.

She placed the broken snow globe carefully on her dresser and walked into her bathroom. She ignored the mess and dug through her drawers looking for the long hair sticks her mom had given her all those years ago.

She tossed out multi-colored ponytail bands until she found what she was looking for, wrapping her fingers around them with a satisfied grin. She rolled the sticks in her hand, remembering how proud she'd been when her mom had given them to her.

They were heavy and long, made of metal with sharply pointed ends, and they had ornate Celtic marks embossed all around them. They were beautiful, just like her mother.

Alder thought she was the weak one, the non-Ellis one, the weak link, the crumbling brick, but she was going to prove him wrong.

She took her hair out of its ponytail and twisted it into a long bun, just like her mom had showed her. When she had it in place she slipped a stick into each side.

She stared at herself in the mirror for a second. She was pale and scared looking, and she had huge black rings under her eyes. She certainly didn't look capable of killing anyone. She looked like a scared little doe. She grinned slightly. If anything, looking like a scared doe was in her favor.

Her stomach growled suddenly, sounding terribly loud in the cavernous bathroom. She hadn't realized how hungry she was. It had been well over a day since she'd eaten. She should probably get some food before she left, but the thought of going back into the kitchen made her feel sick instead of hungry.

Had it really only been three days since they'd all died? It seemed like forever ago. It seemed like it was only yesterday.

She wiped a tear from her cheek and closed her eyes, trying to remember the day before. The day BEFORE the day they'd died. But she couldn't. It was fuzzy in her mind, lost. She thought maybe they'd argued over something silly, like whether or not they should get a new dog.

A floorboard creaked, and Sian spun around. Alder's men were in her bedroom. She snarled angrily, forgetting her plan to hand herself over, and grabbed her hairdryer from the counter.

"You aren't getting THIS Ellis!" she snapped, rushing through the bathroom door and swinging the hair dryer into the nearest one's head, then tackling another and taking him to the floor with a jiu jitsu move.

She crawled onto his chest, slipped her arm through his, and wrenched up until she heard his shoulder snap and his sharp cry of pain.

She rolled quickly to the side, leg-sweeping the man behind her to the floor, breaking his ankle in the process, and then she grabbed his gun and shot the two men still standing in their heads.

She lay there for a second, breathing heavily, feeling a little repulsed that she'd just killed two men. Her eyes narrowed, and her nostrils flared. They had murdered her family. It was no more than they deserved. The two men she'd taken down were moaning in pain, cursing her in accented English. She scrambled to her feet away from them, gun still clutched in her hand.

Until a couple days ago she was an Ellis who had never killed anyone. In three days she'd already killed five men, maybe six. She hadn't been counting, and she frankly didn't care. She'd killed the first men to protect Gavin, and she'd killed these men to protect herself.

But if she shot these other two, the two she'd injured, it would be murder, wouldn't it? She frowned, wondering where the line was. These men were a threat to her family. If she left them, one of them might be the one to kill Gavin or Louise or Nick. She pulled the trigger once, twice, and they were dead.

She grabbed another gun, slipped in into her waistband and ran down the stairs. She skidded to a stop just inside the kitchen door, Crunchy-O's snapping under her shoes. There were more men waiting for her in the kitchen.

Had one of these men killed Owen? Or Mom? Or Danny? Anger rushed through her, devouring her fear. They rushed towards her, and she jumped backwards, pulling her gun and shooting quickly.

Two of them dropped to the floor, but the other three kept coming. Sian dashed out of the kitchen and ran back up the stairs, turning at the top and shooting down the staircase, killing one more.

She bolted down the hallway, but just as she reached her bedroom door, someone grabbed her ankle and pulled, yanking her to the floor. Her chin hit the wooden floor with a hard thud. Pain waved through her jaw and up into her head, and by the time she could think again, he had her in an arm lock.

"I'm not trying to hurt you," he hissed.

She moved her left hand, feeling around for her mace, grinning slightly when she found it. "But I am trying to hurt you," she muttered, ripping the mace upwards and shoving it into his mouth before depressing the trigger. He immediately released her and fell backwards, rolling to his knees, gagging and coughing.

"What the hell did you do, you little bitch?!" the other man yelled when he got to the top of the stairs.

Sian didn't bother to respond, just grabbed her gun, shot them both, and jumped to her feet. She ran into her room and out her open window, shimmying down her tree and dropping to the ground with an "omph".

"Always with the running," Alder said softly. "Women are so predictable. Drop the guns, Sian."

Sian turned slowly. Alder was standing ten feet away, four men flanking him with their guns trained on her.

"Why should I drop them?" Sian snarled. "You want me alive."

"True. But alive and whole are two very different things." Alder smiled as he said it, but it didn't change the cold hardness of his eyes.

Sian's heart pounded. She needed to save Gavin, and the only way to do that was by getting close to Alder. She couldn't get close to him unless she let him take her. And hadn't that been her plan in the first place? She carefully pulled her guns out of her waistband and dropped them to the ground.

"Wise move," Alder said.

Then something hit her from behind, and everything went black.

Chapter Fifteen

Volume 66; Entry 5; **Jack Ellis***:*

If I could live my life over there is only one thing I would change. I do not regret leaving London and my family's legacy behind me. I do not regret all the many lives I have taken. I do not regret the whores or the senators. I do not regret the mine managers or the business owners.

I regret only Bronwen. Without her light to guide me I begin to feel utterly lost. I know the end is coming. I can feel it creeping up on me with feathery feet, and I do not mind. I do not fear death. I never have.

I only wish I knew if Bronwen waited for me on the other side. I only wish I knew if I have completely lost her love.

I sometimes find my socks laid out just the way she would have, and I wonder. Is she here? Is she yet watching over me?

How could she forgive me? How could she still love me? I committed the greatest sin. I refused to let her go free.

Why hasn't she haunted me? Why hasn't she driven me insane with her wails and her terrible moans? How could she have left me? After all I did to keep her.

"We have a problem," Louise said, looking up from her phone.

Gavin sighed. Why couldn't it ever be easy? Why did there always have to be a problem? "What now?" he snapped.

"Pull over."

"I don't need to pull over! Just tell me!"

"Pull the damn car over!"

Gavin ripped the car off the shoulder and slammed the brakes. It skidded towards the edge, and gravel spit everywhere.

"What?!" he yelled.

She handed him the phone, and Gavin tapped the screen. A photo filled it, and he felt the blood drain from his face. He should have known better. He should have never let her go. He should have tied her to a chair in the cabin and left her there.

He punched the send button and waited impatiently for someone to pick up on the other side.

"Gavin Ellis, I presume?" a cultured voice drawled over the line.

"Let her go!"

"No."

"You're going to regret this," Gavin snarled, thinking of a hundred different ways to kill Alder King. A hundred and ten.

"I don't think I will. You see, I think perhaps you are one of the ones."

Gavin fought the urge to shout and ground out, "What ones?"

"The ones who love."

"I don't know what that means."

"You wouldn't. I want the Ellises."

Gavin laughed softly. "Are you sure about that?"

"Sian is sitting here, helpless. At any moment my finger might slip and blow her silly, little brains all over the wall."

Gavin swallowed his rage and said calmly, "And what do you want from me?"

"I want the Ellises. Tied up in a bow on a platter. Better yet, you kill them and bring me their heads, then I'll let Sian go."

Gavin rolled his eyes. King must think he was stupid. There was a bounty out on all the Ellises. ALL the Ellises. And that included Sian. No one was walking away. Least of all King.

"Okay," Gavin said easily.

"Okay what?"

"In exchange for the Ellises on a platter, you'll let Sian go, right?"

"You have my word; do I have yours?"

"Yes; I'll bring you their heads," Gavin said, hanging up before he could hear King's reply.

"New plan," Gavin said, whipping his car around and heading back towards the wooded retreat.

"What?" Nick asked.

"I need Frank's head."

"What?" Louise gasped. "Why?"

"Alder wants heads; he'll get heads."

"I love this new you," Nick said with a laugh.

"I don't!" Louise snapped, holding onto the dash. "I think you're insane!"

Gavin laughed loudly. "Louise, sweetie, all the Ellises are insane. It's our thing."

He used Louise's phone to call Alistair. "Stop on the edge of town and wait for my orders. Pass it on." He didn't wait to hear Alistair's response. Alistair was frightened of him; they all were. They didn't want to end up like Frank, and they knew if they crossed him they would.

He tried not to think of Sian, sitting there, tied to a chair, waiting for him to come. He hoped she knew that no matter what he would always come for her.

King was deranged to think Gavin would trade all the other Ellises for Sian. He would never give up the Ellises, not a single one of them. He was their head; it was his duty to protect them. But Sian was an Ellis too, always had been. And as such it was also his duty to protect her.

Everyone knew you didn't mess with an Ellis. And if you didn't know, you figured it out soon enough. Gavin grinned as he pulled into the driveway. Apparently Alder King was going to have to learn it the hard way.

Alder laughed softly as he slipped his phone into his pocket. "See?" he said, wiping a tear from Sian's cheek. "I told you he loved you more than anyone else. He's willing to give up everyone else for you."

Sian struggled against the ropes holding her to the chair, anger rushing through her. She couldn't believe she'd been so stupid. Gavin would never forgive her if... It didn't bear thinking.

"Buck up," Alder said, lifting her chin. "It won't be long now."

If the gag wasn't so tight in her mouth she would have retched. She'd never felt so helpless. She hated his hands on her face, but there was nothing she could do about it. She'd screwed up again, because there was no way she could kill him if she was tied to a chair.

"Fortunately," Adler said with a smirk, "Your patriarch instilled a heightened sense of honor in his children. 'An Ellis never breaks their word.'" He laughed and added, "And Gavin gave me his word. Now we just wait."

He poured himself a cup of tea, grimaced as he sipped it, and muttered, "I hate this place."

"Do you know the problem with honor?" he asked her suddenly. She glared at him. "You don't? I'll tell you. Honor is like a rope. You're familiar with ropes, yes?"

She wished his tea was poisoned. She wished she could shoot arrows from her eyes. She wanted him dead.

"A rope can be very useful when applied the correct way. For instance, lifting a large parcel. But if you're not careful, it can tie you all up." He jerked on the front of her ropes causing them to tighten over her chest. She gasped behind her gag.

"See?" he whispered. "All tied up, so bound by the concept of your honor you can't actually do anything."

She ignored the wave of blinding dizziness that swept over her and smiled at him around her gag.

He raised an eyebrow. "You disagree?"

She shrugged. He didn't understand one very important aspect about the Ellis family. Honor was everything, but only within the Ellis family. Gavin wouldn't care two pennies about any promise he made to Alder King because King wasn't an Ellis.

She felt a flash of fear. That didn't mean Gavin didn't care about her. She knew Gavin, and she knew he would do anything to save her, and not just because she was an Ellis. She was also his best friend.

She blinked back a tear, wishing she'd never run from him. It had been so stupid to run, so cliché. She'd just been so overwhelmed by everything, so confused. She felt betrayed and lied to. She'd felt wronged. But Gavin had never wronged her. She couldn't believe she'd thought for even a second that he had.

"Although I find your conversation scintillating, I confess I'm a bit bored," Alder drawled, interrupting her thoughts. "Shall I read to you from Jack's journals? There's a particular passage I think you'll find interesting."

Sian shook her head frantically. The last thing she wanted was to learn more about her murderous grandfather.

"I think you'll really enjoy this one. It's one of my favorites, and so applicable to today," Alder said, sitting back in his chair and propping his feet on the desk. He pulled one of the leather volumes from the box on the floor and flipped several pages. "Ah, here it is."

Volume 41; Entry 61; ***Jack Ellis****:*

Henry came to me yesterday with a kill request. I was taken aback at first because he requested permission to eliminate an entire family. My methods have never been that crass. I have only ever eliminated the element or person I deemed unworthy or corrupt.

I immediately demanded that Henry explain the necessity of eliminating the entire family. His argument was so compelling I cannot believe I never thought of it myself.

Sian slammed her back against her chair, pushing it across the hard wooden floor. Alder looked up from the page he was reading with a grin.

"I'm afraid I can't stop yet," he said with a wink. "We're just getting to the good part."

She tried to stamp her feet up and down, anything to block out his words, but she couldn't block a thing. He just kept reading, and the words wiggled their way past all her noise and right into her ears.

Henry wanted to remove a man who had recently moved here from Chicago. On the surface he seems a rather boring man, somewhat off-putting in his manner, but he runs his clothing mercantile efficiently and brings in much fashion and styles from the east coast that the citizens here seem to enjoy.

Henry inadvertently uncovered this man's connection to a gang out of Chicago, and apparently his choosing this location was not a coincidence. They plan to use the store as a hub and further expand their business west.

I despise gangs. They use power and influence to crush the less fortunate under their heel, and they rise to power on the backs of the poor, not so very different from my own father.

Henry explained that removing the father didn't remove the problem. The store would still be here. The wife would run it until the son was old enough to take over, and so on and so forth. Gangs are, after all, a family business.

Alder suddenly started laughing. "That's what Jack created, you know!" he exclaimed after a minute. "The Ellis gang! The irony is so rich I could eat it."

Sian stared at him, wishing she could kick his face in. She despised him. He didn't know anything of family. Her family might be screwed up, they might be misguided, but they were not a gang, and they had NOT built their empire on the backs of the poor. Far from it.

The Ellises had always gone out of their way to help anyone who needed it, to lift others up, to support and protect the less fortunate.

"I'm tempted to remove your gag just to hear your rebuttal," Alder said. "They underestimated you. You have everything it takes to be a true Ellis. I can see it in your eyes."

He took another sip of his tea, then said, "Naturally, since you're only a woman, you're inclined to weakness. But of course that's why I chose you; I knew you would be easy to manipulate."

He shrugged and said, "The Ellises don't seem to mind weakness. Jack actually thought it would make his house stronger to include women. What do you think he'd say if he knew you were its downfall?"

Sian glared at him. She hated how clever his words were, but she knew he was wrong. She wasn't weak. Her family had taught her to be strong. And she wasn't done yet. She would find a way to end this. She would.

"But enough of that. I haven't gotten to the good part yet," he said, picking the journal back up.

We did it together, Henry, his wife, Agnes, and I. We crept in on soft feet. I killed the man where he sat by his desk writing a letter back home. I took more time than I have in years, annoyed at his brazen attempt to strong-arm my citizens. This is my town, my territory.

I'll make sure the letter gets mailed, blood splatter and all. I want to make sure my message is clear. Stay away from here.

Henry killed the wife. He was rather quick about it which surprised me. His methods are usually quite brutal; I've never seen him simply snap someone's neck and be done with it.

Agnes, however, did not make quick work of the children. In the end, Henry stepped in and killed the three of them quickly and without fuss.

I'm not sure what to think of her cruelty. In truth the children were yet innocents. Just like me, they could do nothing to control the family they were born into. I fully understand Henry's logic in removing them, but I cannot say I cared for the look in Agnes's eyes as she dragged them screaming from their beds.

Sian swallowed the bile climbing up her throat, knowing if she threw up into the gag she would choke. She couldn't block the image of it from her mind, couldn't clear her head of the children's screams. Agnes was her great-great grandma. She'd been born of demons.

She felt dizzy just thinking about it. Everyone in her family, her mom, her dad, her siblings, her aunts, uncles, cousins, her grandparents, great-grandparents, great-great grandparents had all been murderers. Every single one of them. It was... It was unfathomable.

What was even more unfathomable is that even knowing it, knowing that they were murderers, didn't change the fact that she loved them. Or the fact that she'd do anything for them.

"Do you think Jack recognized the irony?" Alder asked, pulling the gag from her mouth and holding a glass of water to her lips.

She wanted desperately to knock the water into his face, but her throat was so dry and full of sick, she carefully tilted her head and drank all he would let her.

"So do you?" he asked, hand poised to pull the gag back into her mouth.

"Do I what?" she gasped, hating him more than she'd ever hated anyone.

"Think he recognized the irony?"

She didn't respond, just spit in his face. He laughed softly, pulling the gag back over her lips.

"If you weren't an Ellis, Sian dear," he said wrapping a strand of her hair around his finger. "I think I'd be tempted to keep you."

A wave of revulsion swept through Sian, and she knew with certainty she'd find a way to kill him first. If only she hadn't run from Gavin she wouldn't be here in this stupid mess. She just needed a minute alone so she could get her hands free, and then she'd kill him.

She closed her eyes and breathed deeply. She was right where she wanted to be. She'd planned to be here. She just hadn't planned on being tied up. So now it was a real game of jail break.

She needed a moment alone. That's all she needed. What weapons did she have? What tools could she use? She was a woman. He thought she was inherently weak. So she would be weak.

She gazed at him, trying to make her eyes pleading. He raised an eyebrow. "You're not going to start playing the helpless maiden, are you?" he said with a smirk. "I think we both know better."

She shook her head and continued to stare at him. He lowered her gag. "What?"

"I'm starving," she blurted out, trying to keep her voice wavery and weak. "I haven't eaten in days. Could you at least feed me?"

He started to say something but stopped himself and smiled. "I'll have the boys get you something," he agreed, pulling her gag back up and walking towards the door.

I hate you, Sian thought at his back. I hate you, and I cannot wait to kill you.

Chapter Sixteen

Volume 8; Entry 167; **Edward Ellis***:*

I am troubled. I need to remove Sian, but I am unsure how to do it without also losing Gavin. Although I am still not convinced of Gavin's ability to lead the entire Ellis family, his cousins follow him without question, so I believe when it is his time it is possible he will acquit himself well. But not if he is busy trying to protect Sian.

Gavin, someday you will read this, and you will most certainly be angry with me. You may hate me. I know I have certainly felt my share of hate towards Grandfather.

Understand this, I am your father, and I love you. I love all my children, even Sian. But my responsibility as the head of the Ellis line has and always will come first. I have to consider what is best for everyone not just one of you.

When the day comes that I remove Sian, it is in the best interest of the Ellis family. And whatever is in the best interest of the Ellis family is also your best interest.

As soon as Alder left the room Sian began to work frantically at her knots. It had been a long time since she'd played a game of escape artist, but it was just like riding a bike. Once you knew...

She closed her eyes and felt the knots with her fingers. It felt like a very clumsy handcuff knot. A five year old could make a better knot, she thought with a grin as she started working on it. If they were an Ellis.

It wasn't hard to twist her fingers the way she needed to, and in a matter of seconds she had the knot loose enough to slip her hands out.

She listened carefully, but she didn't hear Alder's footsteps returning so she bent over and started to loosen the knots tying her legs to the chair. Before long she was free.

She quickly took stock of the room, then grabbed the lampstand from the desk. It had a heavy base and was perfect for knocking someone over the head with.

She crept to the door and waited patiently, listening and breathing softly. It wasn't long until she heard footsteps coming down the hallway. She counted. Three. There were three men coming.

She'd let the first one in, bludgeon the second one, and go from there. She waited, heart pounding in her chest, breath coming quickly. The door started to swing open, and she held herself still.

A man stepped through; she let him pass. Another stepped through, and she leaped, bringing the lamp down on his head with as much force as she could. As he dropped to the floor, she grabbed his gun from his belt, shot the man in the hallway and spun around, scrambling backwards to avoid the first man's tackle. She pulled the trigger again, and the man's face exploded into red jelly.

She spun back towards the door, but she was a second too late. Alder winked at her before punching her in the face with enough force to drop her to the floor.

Volume 7; Entry 51; **Henry Ellis:**

I killed Agnes, my wife, the mother of my children, this morning. It was not easy. I should have killed her in her sleep, but I knew I couldn't do it that way. She fought me like a demon. Perhaps she was one. I do not know.

Her blood is still on my hands, marking this page as I write, but I cannot yet clean it off. I cannot yet deal with her body.

She was killing innocents, without permission, with no reason or pure intent. Just killing to kill. I can blame no one but myself. If I had never looked her way, if I had never heard her laugh and thought it sounded like gold on a chain, perhaps she would have remained a simple woman, kneading dough into bread instead of taking lives.

My grief is overwhelming, not that I killed her, but that I made her what she became. I took her to her first kill, taught her how to use a knife, showed her how to take a life.

And I have made my sons and daughters into her as well. They have all held the knife, they have all taken lives, and it is entirely my fault. I am to blame.

It would sometimes be nice if the Ellises weren't so damn efficient, Gavin thought as he worked to dig Frank out of the ground.

"Your turn," he grunted, tossing the shovel to Nick.

"You're wasting time," Louise fumed. "He has Sian!"

"Yes," Gavin said for the sixteenth time. "And if I show up too soon, he'll know I'm not actually handing the Ellises over. This way I can catch him off guard."

"This plan is stupid," she hissed. "He's probably hurting Sian right now."

Gavin's heart thudded. He knew that was true, and he hated thinking of Sian being hurt. But it was a good plan, and he knew Alder wouldn't kill Sian until he had what he wanted. Gavin just had to play it out; it was the only way.

"It'll work," he insisted.

"Got him," Nick said.

"Finally." Gavin grabbed one of Frank's lifeless hands, and together he and Nick pulled Frank out of the loose dirt.

"We should wash him off," Nick suggested. "He looks a little like he's been buried and stuff."

"Louise, grab a bucket of water or something," Gavin ordered. Louise huffed but obeyed.

"What do you make of Alistair?" Gavin asked once Louise was out of earshot.

"He's old. Just making a play for power. He's always wanted more power."

"He and Susan were both on Sian's list."

"Really?"

"Really."

"Who else?"

"Besides you, Louise, Kelly, Frank, and Samuel."

"Sian put Louise on the list?"

"Yeah, something about that guy she was dating a year or so ago."

"Huh. Who do you think it was?"

"I'm not sure. Frank's dead. Alistair and Susan are both acting suspicious. Louise is solid, and I don't see Kelly or Samuel really having the backbone to call down death on the entire family."

"I would add David and Brian."

"I already did."

Nick shrugged. "Then we'll keep an eye on all of them."

Gavin sighed. "I just find it hard to believe anyone in our family could do it. I mean, we're family. How could anyone betray us like this?"

"Maybe they didn't exactly know what would happen," Nick suggested. "And you have to ask yourself why Alder King gives a shit."

"I know," Gavin said, watching Louise return. "I have, and I can't think of a single reason."

They were soon on the road again, Frank's head rolling around on the backseat.

"You could have at least put it in a bag," Louise complained.

"I wanted him to be able to see the view. You know how carsick Frank gets," Gavin said cheerfully.

Nick laughed out loud, but Louise just huffed angrily. "This isn't a joke, you know!" she snapped. "Someone is trying to kill us. Sian, the only one of us who doesn't deserve it, is being held hostage, and FRANK'S HEAD IS IN THE BACKSEAT!!!"

"Relax," Gavin said. "Everything's going to be just fine."

Sian slowly peeled her eyes open. Her head hurt. Her arms hurt. Everything felt strange. She looked up. Her hands were tied above her head, and the rope had been tightened over one of the open rafters. Her fingers were too numb to even feel the knots holding her in place. She couldn't wiggle out of this to save her life.

"You're quite good at this," Alder said from his position behind the desk. "It's really too bad they didn't bring you into the fold."

"Shut up," she hissed, glad he hadn't gagged her again.

"I wouldn't have made that mistake," he added. "Even if you are a woman. It's not the desire to kill that makes you such a powerful weapon. It's your blind loyalty."

He stood and walked towards her. She kicked out at him, gasping as her weight pulled on her shoulders.

He chuckled. "You would do anything to save them. You would happily die; you would commit murder; anything. Anything at all."

"I've never had that problem," he added lazily. "I do what my father tells me to because I know he'll kill me if I don't. Simple. My men follow me because they know I'll kill them if they don't. There is no loyalty. Just fear and hate."

She tried to kick at him again, but the pain was too much. She had to get free. If she didn't Gavin would come, and more than anything she didn't want Gavin to die.

"Here's the difference," Alder said. "If I told you I would walk away in exchange for your life, your body, your wealth and you were actually stupid enough to believe me, you would give it all to me willingly."

He grinned crookedly. "However, if you were holding my father hostage I wouldn't do a thing to save him. In fact, I'd celebrate when you did kill him."

"You're disgusting!" Sian spat, standing on her tiptoes to try to get the feeling back into her hands.

He shrugged. "We're birds of a feather, you and I, both products of our family. You're a product of Jack Ellis's misguided enlightenment, and I'm a product of my father's blind obedience to tradition and blood. In fact, we're cousins, just very far removed."

Sian stared at him, mind totally blank with confusion. He grinned. "Hadn't figured that out yet, had you?"

She still hadn't. "Figured what out?" she asked.

"Jack Ellis, the black sheep. The prodigal son. The heir who never returned," Alder exclaimed grandly. "My great-great grandfather was very put out by living in his older brother's shadow. He resented that he was never the true heir, that his father was always waiting for Jack to return. In fact, I'd say Grandfather hated Jack very, very much. Enough to kill him."

"But..."

"But what? Didn't you realize it when you read the journals? Jack Ellis was the heir to a prominent bloodline. I may not work for the queen, but I have tea with her on occasion. She has a very dry wit."

Alder shrugged. "If it were up to me, I would say let sleeping dogs lie. I don't care that Jack left and never returned. I wouldn't be in line to inherent if he hadn't."

He kicked Sian's feet out, and she yelped in pain as the rope jerked taut on her wrists. "But Father wants you all dead," he whispered in her ear. "So here we are."

Sian struggled to her feet again. Her shoulders hurt so badly she wanted to cry, but she wouldn't. She wouldn't give him the satisfaction.

Alder tucked a loose stand of hair behind her ear. "I did you a favor, you know," he murmured. "Shall I read you the last entry in your father's journal?"

Sian didn't bother shaking her head. She knew he'd read it no matter what.

"Let's see," he said, searching through the journals. "Ah, here it is. The very last words of Edward Ellis."

*Volume 10; Entry 103; **Edward Ellis**:*

I fear I have made another enemy today. Gavin asked that I reevaluate my decision and allow Sian to join the Ellises proper.

Jack must have turned in his grave. Reevaluate? She shouldn't even be here. She should be in Paris or Moscow, snapping photographs, and forgetting the Ellis name.

I told him he was too close to it and he couldn't see Sian honestly, couldn't see who she was. He laughed and said I was a blind fool, and that Sian is as much an Ellis as all the others, maybe even more so.

He has not yet learned to evaluate matters the way that I do. On the surface it is perhaps true that Sian is a perfect Ellis. She is as capable as any Ellis I've ever seen. She is a perfect marksman, an extremely adept fighter, and she wields a knife with ease. I have never once seen her pass up an opportunity to defend an Ellis or anyone else for that matter.

However, what makes her a danger to the Ellis family, what makes it impossible for me to allow her to join us, is her mind. She, more than anyone else, is always questioning. She was the one who asked why we kill deer when we have plenty to eat. She was the one to ask why it's always a single runner in the game and not a gang of runners. She even once asked me why we never leave Colorado! We just don't!

She must always know the why of things. She wants to understand the point of things, the end product, the reason behind the act. She is not inclined towards blind obedience, and THAT makes her a liability.

I have no choice now. I must remove her. If I do not I fear that Gavin will bring her in without permission, and then the entire Ellis line will be in danger.

I dread telling Sylvia. She will not be happy. She is as attached to Sian as Gavin is, and I know she will not support my decision. But if I do not tell her and she was to suspect... I'm not sure any of the Ellis rules would protect me.

Tears poured down Sian's cheeks. She'd wanted to know why he'd excluded her and now she knew. It wasn't that she wasn't good enough, it wasn't that she couldn't hold her own, it wasn't that she wasn't Ellis enough. It wasn't even that she was weak and couldn't stand the sight of blood. It was her nature, her inquisitiveness, her desire to understand the WHY of things.

She wiped her eyes on her shoulder, silently cursing her dad, the man who had made her, the one who had weighed her, found her wanting, and discarded her like a piece of trash.

If only he knew... if only he were still alive she would tell him. She would tell him why she asked questions, why she wanted to know the why of everything.

She'd been about six or so, sitting on the porch with Great-Grandpa Richard. He'd just told her a story about his own grandpa, Jack.

Then he'd wrapped his arm around her shoulders and said, "Let me tell you a secret, Sian my love." She'd leaned in close because he always told the best secrets. "Your great-great-great grandpa Jack was an exceptional man, and do you know why?"

She'd shaken her head and waited for him to tell her. "He was exceptional because he knew when to ask 'why'."

"I don't understand, Grandpa," Sian had said.

"Sometimes in life, Sian, you have to ask why. Why am I doing this? Why is this the right way? Why does this have to be done? And if you can't answer the question, if you don't know the answer, you need to find out. You need to know the why, otherwise you're empty inside, following the beat of someone else's drum."

Sian had made up her mind then and there that she wanted to be exceptional. She wanted to be like her Grandpa Jack. She wanted to be like the man who'd come to a new land and built a legacy his family and his community was proud of. And she had decided that she would always ask why.

And her father had been going to kill her for it. She giggled slightly, suddenly feeling like she was trapped inside a ridiculous horror movie.

"I saved your life," Alder said, scattering her thoughts.

She shrugged, brushed the tears from her eyes again, and smirked at him. "You shouldn't have. You're going to pay for it."

His eyes narrowed, and Sian knew he wanted her to be afraid, but she wasn't. Gavin was coming to get her. The Ellis family was coming to get her.

He grabbed the rope above her wrists and jerked her towards him. "Your life is in my hands," he snarled. "I would watch how you speak to me."

Just as she was going to spit in his face she remembered her mom's words. He'd underestimated her from the beginning, and she wanted to keep it that way, so she dropped her eyes and pretended he had scared her.

"Better," he snapped, releasing her.

She kept her eyes on the floor, knowing if she looked at him he'd see the anger and defiance in her eyes. She needed him to think she was weak. It was the only way she'd ever be able to break free.

Gavin knocked on the door. His heart was pounding like crazy. He'd thought it was a good plan at the time, but as far as plans went it was sketchy at best.

A skinny young man cracked the door open, and Gavin pulled Frank's head from the duffle bag he'd slung over his shoulder and held it up to the crack. The man stepped backward quickly, and Gavin pushed his way in.

"King!" Gavin yelled. "I'm here! I've brought you what you wanted!"

"Gavin Ellis, head of the Ellis clan, how delightful to finally meet you," a voice drawled from a doorway nearby.

Gavin turned towards the voice, resisting the urge to drop Frank's head, pull his gun, and shoot King full of lead. He was sick of games, but he needed to see Sian before he could end it.

"Where's Sian?" Gavin demanded.

"Safe," King replied. "I see one head only. I demanded all the heads."

"I have them," Gavin snapped. "Where's Sian?"

"Bring the head here," King said, stepping back into the room but leaving the door open.

Gavin walked forward, irritation crawling down his spine. He would never normally let an enemy be at his back. He wished he could just kill everyone and be done with it. It wasn't going to be as simple as that though. He'd already counted fifty-seven men, and he knew there were more.

He stepped into the room and froze, adding another fifteen ways to his list of how he might kill King. "Sian," he whispered, fighting the urge to run forward and free her.

Her face was pale and tight with pain. The skin around one eye was dark blue, and he could tell she'd been crying. He promised himself he would bruise King just as much, all over his body. He'd bruise him, then rip his heart from his chest.

He tried to catch her eye, but her eyes were glued to his hand, glued to Frank's dead head.

"You didn't," she gasped.

"He started it," Gavin said, grinning to let her know it was all okay.

"It seems you have actually brought me an Ellis," King said, lips tweaked into a smirk, hand on Sian's shoulder.

Gavin would tear that hand from King's body. He would rip it off and every other body part that had touched Sian. He would take his time. He would kill King as slowly as possible.

"They're in the truck," Gavin said dismissively, struggling to keep himself under control.

"All of them?" King asked in disbelief.

"All of them. I'm the head of the Ellises," Gavin said, infusing his voice with power. "I said 'get in the back of the truck', and they did. Then I mowed them all down with a machine gun. Count them; you'll see they're all there."

Sian just stared at him, forehead wrinkled in confusion.

"What did I tell you, Sian dear?" Alder said with a grin. "Man of his word."

"I'd do anything to protect Sian," Gavin declared. "Anything."

"I thought you would," Alder said, face lined with disgust. "Love," he spat. "It's a crippling emotion."

Gavin stared at Alder intently. He was playing a deep game now, and he couldn't afford to be distracted. He couldn't get drawn into a conversation or make light of the situation. He needed Alder to think he was dead serious.

"Let her go!" he demanded.

"Let's count them first," King replied.

Gavin swallowed his smile. "By all means."

"After you," King said, gesturing towards the door.

Gavin didn't even glance at Sian on the way out. He couldn't risk it. He couldn't risk giving anything away.

Sian swallowed a sob. Frank was dead, and Gavin had killed him. She didn't overly much care about Frank. He was one of the few Ellises she hadn't actually liked, but she couldn't believe that Gavin had killed him for her. And she didn't believe for a second that he'd killed all of the Ellises. She just couldn't.

As soon as Alder stepped through the door, Sian took a deep breath and hoisted herself upright, grabbing the ropes she dangled from. Pain washed over her, but she ignored it. She couldn't be weak right now. She had to be strong.

She jerked, pulling herself up and over, until she could wrap her legs around the ropes and hold herself there without putting pressure on her wrists.

She pulled her hands together and began to work frantically on the knots, using her fingers and her teeth. She had to get free. Gavin's deceit would be revealed soon enough, and Alder would kill him and then return to kill her. She had to save Gavin. Had to. He was all she had left.

The knot loosened, and she jerked at it, pulling one hand loose and starting to work on the other. Just another minute and she would be free.

Chapter Seventeen

*Volume 31; Entry 310; **Jack Ellis**:*

If I have learned anything over the years it is this: never underestimate your opponent. Most of my targets never even see me coming. They never know that death is on their doorstep. But every now and then, someone will surprise me.

It vexes me that after all these years I can still be caught off guard. It seems as if I should have seen it all, done it all, dealt with it all, expect it all.

However, I suppose there is some relief in knowing that I am not all-knowing, that I can be surprised, that I am only human.

Gavin Ellis wasn't as smart as Alder had thought he was. He had actually killed his entire family to protect his weak, stupid sister. What a tiresome and pathetic move.

It left Alder with a vile taste in his mouth, one he didn't quite understand. What was the point in sacrificing so much for one person? Especially when they both had to know they were going to die anyway. What part of "all the Ellises" could they not get through their thick skulls?

Alder walked carefully behind Gavin, leaving at least ten feet between them. The sooner he could shoot him in the head and be done with it, the happier he'd be. He was ready to go home. He hated it here. He was even beginning to hate the Ellises, although not nearly as much as his father did.

He stopped and studied the large box truck, trying to decide if eighty-odd people would have been able to fit inside. He took note of the multitude of bullet holes riddling the truck walls. Then he stared at the head hanging loosely from Gavin's hand. He watched a fly buzz around it a few times and finally land in the open mouth. He was certain it was an Ellis head. Sian's reaction had been too expressive and real.

They deserved it really, the Ellises. They were crass and coarse. Worst of all they had turned on the members of their own class. One would never know they had descended from one of the most imperial lines of England. Too much trash blood mixed in. Even imperial blood couldn't blot out the blood of a whore.

Alder shook his head. He could reflect on this whole filthy business later, on his way home. "Open the door," he ordered Gavin.

Gavin turned and held out the head. "You want to hold this for me?"

"No," Alder growled.

Gavin shrugged, dropping the head on the pavement and stepping forward to open the truck.

If it was wired to explode, Alder didn't think Gavin would be so willing to open it. But one never did know. He took several careful steps backwards and watched intently as Gavin keyed in the combination for the padlock. Then the truck door rolled up, and all hell broke loose.

Sian had just gotten free and dropped to the floor when the explosion happened. She quickly covered her head and ducked behind Alder's desk, waiting for the house to fall down around her ears.

But the explosion didn't stop, and the house didn't fall. That's when Sian realized the noise was actually gunfire. "Gavin!" she gasped, jumping to her feet and dashing towards the door.

Several of Alder's men were running towards the front door, and Sian tackled one, taking him to the ground, breaking his arm, and ripping his gun from his hand. She shot the man in his chest, then spun around and shot two of the other men in the back.

She felt a brief moment of regret. Somebody, somewhere, had a rule about shooting people in the back, but she was sure it wasn't an Ellis family rule, and right now she just needed to win.

She bolted forward, pushing the door open, then skidded to a halt. The Ellises were pouring out of the back of a huge truck, guns blazing, faces hard as granite.

Sian just stood there watching them, feeling a bit of shock that this was actually her family. Alistair was shooting two guns at once; Nick was firing an assault rifle; Louise had a double barreled shotgun. Some of Sian's younger cousins were working together, back to back, firing in bursts. They were all here. Her family. Her crazy, insane, murderous family.

"I can't believe this," Sian whispered, watching Alder's men fall all over the courtyard. She scanned the yard, looking for Gavin's reddish, blond hair. If he was dead she would never forgive herself.

Relief flooded her when she saw him up against the wall, tearing into Alder, knife flashing. Alder was holding his own, which surprised her. During their many pretend gladiator matches among the cousins, Gavin had never lost a knife fight.

She started to run towards them but jumped backwards, heart pounding as a bullet tore into the ground in front of her feet. She ducked behind a column, gasping in surprise as hot pain sliced through her shoulder.

She rolled instinctively to the side, dodging the next knife strike of the man who'd snuck up behind her. She pulled her gun up, aimed, and pulled the trigger, shooting him in the chest. He jerked backwards but fell forward, collapsing on her and pinning her to the ground.

Sian struggled to push his dead weight off her, gagging as his warm blood oozed all over her face. Just when she felt like she might pass out, the weight suddenly lifted, and Nick pulled her to her feet.

"You okay?" he asked. She nodded. "Don't get yourself killed out here," he said, grinning a bit.

"I won't," she replied, feeling awkward because she knew now, and he knew she knew.

"Good," he replied, shooting over her shoulder. "Nice to see you."

"Are we making conversation?" Sian asked with a laugh, pulling him to the side and shooting three men who ran into the courtyard from the front door.

"Sure." He winked at her, then pulled a baton and ran towards a group of men who had cornered one of Sian's uncles.

Sian watched him bludgeon one of Alder's men, then put her back to a porch column as she searched for Gavin again. There was so much going on. Everywhere Alder's men and the Ellises were fighting, trying to gain control.

Several Ellises were using a flower bed as cover to fire on a group of Alder's men. Another group had some of Alder's men penned down in the garage. Everywhere she looked there was blood and guns and people dying.

Her heart thudded anxiously. She didn't see Gavin anywhere. A man rushed her, and she fired at him, gasping in surprise when nothing happened. She jumped to the side just in time, and his knife barely missed her chest but caught on her sleeve.

She ripped her sleeve loose and backed away quickly as he moved towards her. She was out of bullets, and he had a knife. Uncle Danny had always told her the only defense against a knife was a gun.

She stepped back again, knowing it was just a matter of time before he rushed her. She tried to remember what she'd done the one time she'd lost her knife play fighting Owen. He'd had her backed against a wall, but she'd still won. How had she done it?

She suddenly smiled, remembering exactly what she'd done, then she dropped to the ground and rolled quickly towards his legs like a log. When she hit his legs, he stumbled forward, and she swiftly mounted his back before he could recover.

She grabbed the hand he was holding his knife with, pulled it towards herself, then shoved the knife deep into his neck. Using all her weight, she pushed the knife back out, ripping his throat in half. Blood spewed all over the stones, and his body shuddered once, then went still.

Sian grabbed his gun from his waistband, checked it for bullets, and quickly stood, searching for Gavin once more. This time she saw him. He and Alder were rolling across the ground, knives flashing in the sunlight.

Alder suddenly broke free and jumped to his feet. Sian gasped as she watched him dive at Gavin, but Gavin rolled away, and in a second they were both on their feet again, moving back and forth.

She wanted to help Gavin, but she couldn't really. He was fighting hand to hand, and if she tried to help him she'd only get in his way.

She was trying to figure out a different way to help when she saw one of Alder's men trying to sneak up behind Gavin. She pulled her gun up, sighted down the barrel, and shot him in the head. She may not be able to help Gavin, but she could damn well make sure nobody helped Alder either.

She ran to the next column and braced her back against it, trying to watch everyone in the courtyard all at once. Her eyes caught a movement up on the roof, and she followed it. A man with a rifle was sighting in on Gavin. She took aim and fired. The man yelped in surprise, then tumbled from the roof, his head breaking open on the paving stones.

Sian stepped forward again, only to stop. Her cousin Judy lay dead on the ground in front of her, forehead open like a broken pomegranate.

Judy was only nineteen. She was sweet and funny. She liked riding bikes on the trails. She was a good singer. She and Sian had gone hiking just last week.

Alder would pay. They would all pay, Sian thought, rage consuming her. Nobody messed with the Ellises. Nobody.

Gavin jumped forward, thrusting his knife towards King's heart. He hadn't expected him to be such a good fighter, but in a way he was glad. He would have been disappointed to just kill him quickly and be done with it. This way he could take a piece at a time. This way he could make him pay.

King dodged to the side and slashed out with his own knife, but Gavin easily evaded it, slicing his knife across the back of King's hand. Blood welled, and King dropped back, moving his knife to his other hand.

"When I'm done with you," he snarled, eyes hard, "I'm going to kill your sister. Very, very slowly."

Gavin didn't bother to respond. King wasn't going anywhere near Sian, not ever again. He feinted forward, anticipating King's block and knocking King's arm to the side, then he slid under King's guard and thrust his knife towards his ribs.

Just before his knife made contact, Gavin caught a flash of blond from the corner of his eye and turned his head slightly to follow it. Sian was running like a demon across the courtyard. One of Alder's men tried to stop her, and she didn't even pause, just shot him and kept running. But on the other side of the courtyard, Alistair was watching Sian, and he was slowly raising his gun and sighting down the barrel.

"Hell!" Gavin hissed, pushing King's hand away, flinching slightly as King's knife grazed his ribs. Gavin kicked King in the knee, shoving him away, and bolted across the courtyard towards Sian.

"SIAN!" he yelled. "Forward breakfall!"

She didn't hear him, and Gavin kept running. He saw the moment Alistair started to pull the trigger, and Gavin dived forward, reaching out and ripping Sian to the ground.

Gavin rolled to his back, grabbed Sian's gun from her hand, and shot Alistair in the head three times as he tried to bolt for the gate. Alistair dropped to the ground like a stone.

Sian groaned beneath him, and Gavin rolled to his knees. "Sian? Are you okay?"

He started to move her, searching for blood, but she batted his hands away. "What the hell're you doing?" she snapped.

"Saving your life," he replied. "Again."

She laughed. "No; I'm saving your life." Her face sobered. "I'm so sorry, Gavin. I shouldn't have run." She launched herself forward, wrapping her arms around his waist. "I missed you. I'm sorry. I don't care, not about any of it. I love you. All of you."

Gavin hugged her back, feeling such acute relief he almost cried. Hot liquid suddenly splattered over his face, and one of King's men dropped to the ground beside them.

Gavin pushed her back and grinned. "Now's probably not the time. We've got to finish this."

She smiled shakily at him. "I was heading for the roof. There's a rifle up there."

"I'll give you a boost."

They ran the rest of the way to the house together, killing any of King's men they passed on the way. As soon as they reached the wall, Sian stepped onto Gavin's knee, and he launched her upwards. She grabbed the edge of the roof and quickly shimmied up onto it. She turned and gave him a thumbs up, then scrambled across the roof.

Gavin turned back towards the courtyard. He could see the Ellises were winning, but it hadn't been an easy fight. He searched the standing faces for King, but he didn't see him. He hissed in frustration. It wouldn't be over until King was dead.

Alder limped quickly across the courtyard. He hated the Ellises. Every single one of them. He didn't care if he had to hire all the hitmen in America, he was taking them out one way or another.

He stepped over his younger brother's body, kicking him as he did, and made his way towards the SUV's. Right now retreat was the best option. Then he'd figure out a way to kill them once and for all.

He flattened up against the wall as a tall woman struggled against one of his men and sighed in irritation when she pulled a knife from her boot and shoved it halfway through his man's throat. So maybe the Ellises were a little more trained than he'd given them credit for.

Alder moved forward, wrapped his arm around the woman's waist and placed his own knife to her throat. She hissed angrily and started to spin, but he tightened his hold.

"Don't struggle," he ordered. "Move towards the SUV."

She stood rigid for a moment, then stepped carefully forward. "Good," he said. "I'm going to let go of you, but my gun is pointed at your spine. Keep going, quickly now, and get in the passenger side."

She glanced sideways, and he figured she was evaluating her chances. She must have decided they weren't good, because she jogged forward and hopped into the SUV with no argument.

"There's a pack of zip ties under the seat," he said, holding his gun steady on her from six feet away. "Put one around your wrists and tighten it down with your teeth."

She glared at him for a second, and he wished she would hurry. The constant gunfire and yelling was starting to grate on his nerves, but just when he'd decided to shoot her, she pulled out a zip tie and tightened it down.

He grinned at her, slammed her door shut, and jumped into the driver's seat. He started the engine, backed over three of his own men, and peeled out of the courtyard, leaving Gavin Ellis and his filthy clan behind him.

Sian scrambled across the roof tiles. The man she'd killed had fallen, but his rifle was still balanced precariously on the roof edge, and if she could get to it, she could even the odds a bit.

She lay on her stomach and reached towards it. Just a little further, she thought, scooting forward and stretching, gasping in relief when her fingers touched the strap. She curled her fingers around it and pulled it towards her, then she sat up and crawled several feet further up the roof.

She settled her feet against the tile and turned to survey the courtyard. It would be harder to aim without an object to brace the rifle on, but she didn't dare take the time to climb to the top of the roof. She checked the chamber, saw it was loaded, then brought the rifle up to her shoulder.

It had been several years since she'd shot a rifle, but she could still remember her Uncle Danny's quiet instructions. She could remember his hands moving her head to the right angle.

"This is for you, Uncle Danny," she whispered as she sighted one of Alder's men through the scope. She squeezed softly, and the rifle fired, the retort echoing off the courtyard walls, shocking her with its loudness.

The man's head exploded, and he dropped to the ground. Sian repositioned the rifle and searched for another target. A man's head popped up in the garage window, and Sian sighted in on him, pulling the trigger softly, ready for the recoil and retort now, not even flinching when the rifle slammed back into her shoulder.

She sighted again, pulling the trigger again and again. An engine roared, and she swung the rifle towards the sound. She saw a glimpse of Alder's face and just the side of Louise's before a black SUV roared towards the gates of the courtyard.

"Louise!" she gasped. She fired into the back window, aiming for the driver's seat. The window exploded, but the car kept driving. She sighted carefully and pulled the trigger again, but nothing happened.

She glanced down. The clip was empty. "Shit!" she hissed.

Alder was getting away, and he had Louise. She scrambled towards the edge of the roof, searching for a way to get down. She was too far off the ground to jump without something soft to land on, but there wasn't a single soft patch of grass. She finally turned and ran up the roof, breaking out a skylight and dropping into a room on the second story.

She dashed out of the room and down the stairs, careening through the front doors back into the courtyard. But once she was there she forgot about Alder and Louise for a moment. The courtyard was quiet and covered in bodies and blood. The very air felt heavy and thick. The fight was over. And the Ellises had won.

Chapter Eighteen

Volume 66; Entry 25; **Jack Ellis***:*
I stand in awe of the legacy I will soon leave behind. My children have children, and those children have children, and even a few of those children have children. There are so many of them, and they are all pure-bred Ellises.

We gathered together today, and I watched them with joy. The responsibility of being Ellises has not destroyed them. They are strong, yet they still know how to laugh, how to enjoy a moment, how to love.

I am proud of what I have created. I can look at it and say "It is good".

The sun was low in the sky, and golden light filled the courtyard, highlighting every single drop of blood. She couldn't believe they'd done this. Her family had done this. How had she never known what they were?

She felt a wave of grief, knowing they'd lost even more Ellises today, knowing their family was that much smaller. But they had won. They had fought, and they had won. They hadn't just hid in holes in the ground, waiting for death to find them. They had faced it on their own terms.

She smiled, feeling a strange sense of pride. This was her family. This was Jack's legacy. They were survivors.

They were whatever they needed to be. Then she remembered Louise.

"Gavin!" she yelled. "Where are you?"

The remaining Ellises turned to look at her. Their faces were grim, and Sian didn't know what to say to them. They had known, all this time they had known, and she hadn't. But it wasn't about her right now.

"Gavin!!" she yelled again.

Gavin stepped around the truck and headed towards her, relief clear on his face. "Sian," he laughed, hugging her tightly.

"Gavin, Alder's gone; he took Louise. We have to follow him."

"Not yet. I need to deal with this."

"But Gavin..."

"Sian! I'm the head of the Ellises. I'm the leader. My word is law. You don't know; you weren't taught, but I need you to shut up and listen."

She stared at him in disbelief. His voice was stern, and his face had a seriousness to it that looked completely out of place. Where had this Gavin been? Where had he been hiding?

Gavin stepped forward. "Ellises! We have won this fight, yet we have not won the war. King escaped, taking one of our own with him, and do you know why?"

No one said a word. Sian saw uncertainty flicker across some of the faces and realized they were scared of him. The Ellises were scared of her brother.

"Betrayal! That's why!" Gavin snarled. "Nick, bring me Susan."

Someone in the crowd gasped, and Sian assumed it was Susan. She wanted to tug on Gavin's arm and tell him what Alder had said about the newspaper, but his face was so stern she didn't dare.

She'd seen her dad standing in front of the Ellises before. She'd seen how they hung on his every word, and she hadn't understood. But she did now. Gavin held the life of every single Ellis in the palm of his hand. His word determined whether they lived or died. It was terrifying.

The Ellises parted, and Nick walked out, dragging Susan with him. She reached for her husband's hand as she passed him, but he stepped back, face hard.

"I didn't do it!" she screamed. "I didn't do anything!"

"Susan Ellis," Gavin declared. "I am charging you with treason."

"Treason?" Susan sputtered. "You're insane! You're all insane! You can't charge a family member with treason!"

Gavin shrugged one shoulder. "The Ellises can. What did you and Alistair plan?"

She paled slightly and muttered, "Nothing."

"Try again. I saw you talking with him, and he tried to kill Sian."

Sian's eyes widened, and she gasped, "When?"

"While I was fighting King. He took a shot at you while you were running for the roof."

So that's why Gavin had tackled her and also how Alder had gotten away.

"You're a terrible Ellis," Susan spat. "And you'll be a worthless leader, always trying to protect poor little Sian! Alder King would be dead if it wasn't for her! And then the Ellises would be protected!"

Sian shook her head in disbelief. Susan had gone from being mousy and scared to acting like a hateful shrew.

She glanced past Susan to see what the other Ellises thought of Susan's accusation and saw they had distanced themselves from her, offering no support.

"From the outside perhaps," Gavin said, tone hard as steel. "If I hadn't stopped Alistair, who would he have killed next? Nick? Louise? David? Me? That was the plan wasn't it? Remove me so Alistair could take control."

Susan's eyes widened, and she swallowed nervously as if suddenly realizing her precarious position. "I don't know," she mumbled. "He didn't say. I mean, he wanted control, but he didn't say anything about killing anyone."

Gavin smiled slightly. "There's no other way to take control. Susan Ellis, you have been found guilty."

Sian didn't even get the chance to whisper "no". Susan's head exploded, and blood sprayed all over the Ellises standing behind her.

"I AM THE HEAD OF THIS FAMILY!!!" Gavin yelled, gun still held out before him. "DOES ANYONE ELSE WISH TO QUESTION ME?!!" No one responded. No one even moved.

Sian stared in shock. This couldn't be her family. This couldn't be her brother. He... He... He had shot Susan in the head. He'd executed her like she was some kind of criminal.

Sian frowned. They were. They all were. They were murderers. She was drowning in confusion. She loved them. She loved Gavin. She had watched him blow Susan's head off, and she still loved him.

"King has Louise," Gavin continued. "I'm going to find her. In the meantime, I want you all to clean up this mess. Nick's in charge."

Nick nodded, and Gavin grinned at him. "Put all King's men inside the house and burn it. Take the Ellises out with the truck. I'll let you handle the details there."

"Makes sense," Nick said flippantly. "I am the coroner after all."

"Oh, and search the house before you burn it. The locals King was holding hostage might still be alive. If they are, make sure they understand what's expected of them."

Nick nodded, and Gavin turned back to his family. "When everything's done, I want everyone to return home. I'll let you know when King is dead, and Louise is safe." There were a few murmurs of assent.

"Are you sure Alistair and Susan were the ones?" Nick asked Gavin quietly.

"I'm sure they were taking advantage of the situation, but I'm not sure they were the ones. I am sure that if the traitor is still alive they're scared to their marrow and won't ever do anything so stupid again." Gavin frowned. "We lost a good handful to this debacle, and why?"

"I'm not sure one of the Ellises betrayed us," Sian said softly, still a little astounded at Gavin's new role.

"What do you mean?" he asked.

"Alder said one of his tech guys found an article about the Ellis family and they identified Jack from that."

"But why do they care?" Nick demanded.

"I'm a little unclear, but I think Jack was the heir to a noble bloodline in England, and apparently his younger brother nursed a hatred of Jack. Alder is Jack's brother's descendent."

"Seriously?" Gavin said, tone full of disbelief.

"Seriously."

"That's the stupidest thing I've ever heard!" he snapped. "You're saying King's family has been carrying a grudge for almost a hundred and fifty years, and once they found us they thought they'd just go ahead and wipe out our entire line?"

"I guess?" Sian said. "That's what Alder said."

"No wonder Jack left," Nick snorted.

"I've got to go find King," Gavin said.

"I'll go with you," Sian insisted.

"No..."

"Yes. We stick together. Crap happens when we separate."

"That's true. I should really make you take the oath though."

"There's an oath?"

Gavin shrugged and said, "All the Ellises swear allegiance to the Ellis family, to abide by the rules, and to obey the head."

Sian's eyes narrowed. "The head being you?"

"Yep."

"Nope; not doing it."

"You can't just not do it."

"Can. Here's the thing," Sian said. "You know I love you. I love all the Ellises. I've killed enough people the last couple days to prove that. You'll always have my loyalty, but I'm not taking an effing oath."

"The whole thing falls apart if even one of us doesn't follow the rules," Gavin said.

"The whole thing should fall apart!" Sian snapped. "Being a family is one thing, deciding who should live or die based on arbitrary crap is another! You're the head now, so it's up to you, isn't it? To decide who to kill and who does it?" Sian demanded, feeling absolutely disgusted by the whole ordeal.

"So when Jilly's old enough to kill someone," she whispered, thinking of Nick's cheerful daughter, "you're just going to pick some random person for her to kill? Have I got it right?"

Chapter Nineteen

*Volume 25; Entry 155; **Henry Ellis**:*
I thought today was going to be a very bad day indeed. After much careful evaluation, I gave Edward permission to bring Sylvia into the fold, if of course she accepted his proposal.

Naturally she did, after which he explained the Ellis family and what would be expected from her. She accepted everything readily except one thing. The oath.

She and Edward argued for hours, and I began to worry that I would have to kill her. I have always liked Sylvia, and I believe she will be an asset to the Ellis family especially Edward, but not if she refuses the oath.

A family such as ours can only have one leader, and I am he. Everyone else must accept my rule, my direction, my word as law, or it all falls apart.

Gavin stared into Sian's flashing eyes. He could feel the Ellises moving behind him, carrying bodies and picking up guns; he could feel Nick watching him; he could feel Sian's anger. And he hated it.

He'd never wanted this. He'd never wanted to be head of the Ellises; it's just the way things were. He'd never had a choice. He was the heir.

He didn't really mind killing people, especially if they had it coming. Just a couple weeks ago he'd killed a slumlord who refused to update any of his apartment buildings. He and the leasees were headed towards a long legal battle; meanwhile a kid had died two months earlier because one of the stair railings had popped off.

Gavin hadn't minded killing the landlord at all. But he hadn't picked him. His dad had said, "Gavin, do this", and Gavin had done it. Sian was right. He honestly didn't want to be the one to say "Jilly, do this".

Jilly was Nick's oldest daughter. She was only six, and she was a happy, wild child. She never won any of the games the kids played because she could never stop laughing long enough to really participate.

Gavin closed his eyes, imagining all of Nick's children with real knives in their hands, slicing some dirty politician's throat in a filthy alley somewhere. Then he saw them running through a vineyard, hair streaming behind them, shrieking with laughter, grape juice staining their toes.

He looked at Nick. Nick's eyes were clouded, but he shrugged as if to say "it is what it is". But was it? Did it have to be?

"I need to find King," Gavin said, knowing that was at least one thing he was comfortable saying needed done. "Nick, take care of this. Sian, come with me."

"Eddie," he said as he passed one of the younger Ellises. "I need you."

Eddie dropped the body he was helping carry and trotted after Gavin. "Whadda you need?"

"That car," Gavin said, pointing towards one of the SUV's.

"I can do that," Eddie said with a grin as he pulled out his phone and headed for the driver's side.

"What's he doing?" Sian asked.

"Not sure. At a guess I'd say hacking into the car."

"He can do that?"

"I think Eddie can pretty much do anything if it's connected to a computer."

"Wow! I knew he was nerdy, but... wow."

"Yeah, he's handy."

"Got it!" Eddie said with a quick grin.

"Can you track Louise's phone?" Gavin asked.

"Yeah; easy."

"Get in the back and tell me where to go."

"Okay."

"He's good," Sian whispered.

"The best," Gavin agreed, pulling out of the courtyard and heading back towards town.

"Turn left," Eddie ordered. "Then right. Then back towards Golden."

They drove silently for a while, and Gavin wished Sian would say something, anything. He wished he knew what she was thinking. He wished he knew if she was mad at him.

She'd been through so much. Not only had her family just been murdered, but she'd also just found out her entire family was lying to her. And that they were a highly skilled, highly trained... He couldn't think of any other word but "gang". They were a gang with a very specific set of rules. They weren't out to hurt people or gain power. They were out to make things better.

He tried to remember how he'd reacted when his dad had first told him. He'd laughed, but it hadn't taken him long to realize his dad was serious. Then he'd felt a whole rush of emotions. Confusing emotions. Mostly fear. Fear that they would all get caught and sent to jail forever.

But then he remembered that his Uncle Fred was the chief of police. And three of his dad's cousins were local judges. So he'd moved on from fear to disbelief. How could they just go around killing people? And how did they pick? Did they just pull names from a hat? His dad had explained all that, but he hadn't been there to explain it to Sian.

"Do you have any questions?" Gavin asked awkwardly.

"Questions? About what?"

"The Ellises. How we work? What we do?"

"Oh I think I have a pretty good grasp," she said, voice thick with irritation.

"Are you sure?"

"Let's see, you have an arbitrary set of rules that people should live by. When people don't follow these made up and invisible rules, you decide they are corrupt and kill them. Is that about right?"

He started to argue, then frowned. "Actually, that's about the sum of it."

"Why?" Sian demanded. "Why did you do it?"

"Because he told me to."

"So! Why not say no?!"

"I really couldn't," Gavin whispered, feeling a little broken inside. For the first time in her life Sian didn't idolize him. He wasn't her hero.

"I'm sorry," Sian replied softly. "I know you couldn't. No one could. And if he'd asked me, I would have too. You know I would have." She looked out the window and shook her head.

"It makes me so mad!" she snapped suddenly. "He didn't include me, and he should have! He was actually going to kill me! Alder read me his last journal entry. Dad had made up his mind. He would have killed me that day or the next. I don't know. Alder saved my life. But..."

She didn't go on, and Gavin knew she was remembering Owen, Alice, and Mom. He knew she was regretting the cost.

He felt a moment's disgust at himself for being glad, but he pushed the disgust aside. He wanted Owen and Alice, Mom and Grandma back. He missed them. But if he could only have one, he was glad it was Sian.

"Are you sure Dad was going to kill you?" he asked, feeling a little horrified she'd been so close to dying. "What if Alder was lying to you?"

"No," she replied, shaking her head. "It sounded like Dad. He said he had to figure out a way to tell Mom and that he didn't think she'd take it well." She paused, then whispered, "He said she loved me."

"Of course she did!" Gavin exclaimed. "We all do. Did... All of us. Dad, Owen, Alice, Grandma, Uncle Danny, Nick, Louise. We love you! That's why it was so hard to let you go."

She shook her head and said softly, "But you should have let me go."

His heart seized, and he felt such guilt. He'd been the one to keep her. He shouldn't have. He should have let her go. He should have let her be free. How could he have stopped her from living her life?

"It would have been easier on all of you," she whispered.

He glanced at her, surprised. She wasn't blaming him for ruining her life. She wasn't blaming him for anything. She'd just said it would have been easier on all of them. But it wouldn't have been. He opened his mouth to tell her so, but Eddie interrupted.

"They've stopped," Eddie said from the backseat. "They stopped at... huh..."

"What?" Gavin snapped. "Where are they?"

"Your house," Eddie said softly.

"Oh. Great."

Beside him Sian shuddered, but Gavin figured it made sense to end it there. He would kill King in Jack's house, and then it would be done. King would be dead, and everything could go back to normal. If that's what he wanted.

It was all he knew; all he'd ever known. The idea that it didn't have to be that way had never really occurred to him. The Ellises were different. They always had been.

For one, they had money and a lot of it. For two, they all stayed together. He knew every single Ellis's name and birthday and likes and dislikes.

He relived that moment, seeing Susan's eyes darken right before he blew out her brains. She'd known she was going to die, and she had been scared. He'd almost stopped himself. He'd almost folded, but he hadn't.

It had hurt him to kill her. He'd actually liked Susan. She had a strange sense of humor, and she often texted him odd little GIFs of dancing animals. But he couldn't let even the smallest bit of disloyalty slide. It put all the Ellises in danger.

"It's for the good of the Ellises," his father's voice said in his head. "All the Ellises, not just you."

"But Sian belongs!" Gavin had argued. "She's one of us!"

"She's not! I can see it."

His father was right; Gavin could finally see it. Sian wasn't one of them; she wasn't a true Ellis. She could kill just as well as any of them, she was loyal through and through, and she never broke her word.

But what made her dangerous, what made her an outsider, a risk, was that she was the only one to ever question, to ask why, to think maybe there was another way, to refuse to take the oath. His father, in his own misguided way, had only been trying to protect the bulk of the Ellises.

Gavin couldn't do it. He couldn't make those decisions. He couldn't tell Nick to send Jilly away. He couldn't tell Louise she couldn't marry whoever she wanted. He couldn't. He loved them, and he wanted them to be happy. All of them.

Did that make him a traitor? He was the head of the Ellises. If he didn't believe in the rules, if he didn't follow them, how could he enforce them? And how could he turn his back on everything his ancestors, his own father, had worked so hard to build?

"Gavin?"

Gavin glanced at Sian, then back out the window. "What?" he growled.

"I'm sorry I argued with you."

"Which time?"

"All of them. No, I mean, I'm not. I guess I shouldn't have argued with you in front of Nick; I wasn't thinking. I know that a leader can't be questioned in front of his band. Dad always said that; I just didn't realize how he meant it."

Gavin laughed sharply. "Dad said lots of things."

"Why didn't you just let him send me away?"

"Did you want to go?" he asked, tone reserved.

"No! But wouldn't it have been easier?"

"No."

He didn't go on, and Sian watched his face. He didn't look anything like the Gavin she knew. He looked... like their dad. Serious, unyielding, hard. She hated it.

His face suddenly softened, and he grinned. "No, it wouldn't have been easier. Not at all. You were worth every fight, every look, every murmur of discontent." He winked at her. "You're my baby sister. I couldn't stand the thought of you being sent away and never seeing you again. You've always been my best friend. Always."

He shrugged his one shouldered shrug and said, "And I like this. You and I hunting down the bad guy together. We could have always been doing this."

She shook her head. "I don't think we could have."

"You're probably right," he said after a minute. "Dad always said you didn't belong. I thought it was because you didn't like blood and killing things; but I saw how you could really be, and I knew you didn't have any problem protecting people."

"That's not what this is," Sian argued.

"It really is. You may not see it that way, but we've done a lot of good."

"Yeah, but what about..."

"What about what?" Gavin asked.

"Justice, morality, checks and balances."

"It's all there. Anyone has a right to challenge a kill, but it rarely happens. Morality is just a made up word. Jack once said that the definition of wrong is so easily changeable that it doesn't actually exist."

Sian opened her mouth to argue, but Gavin kept going, "And justice, where's the justice in a system that locks a guy up for years for selling drugs to people who ask for them but releases a murderer-rapist in under five years? How is that justice?"

"I don't know, but you don't just get to decide!"

"We actually do. Do you remember that teacher who raped all those students? He threatened to get them expelled if they didn't do what he wanted?"

She nodded. It had turned into national news because one of the girls had finally come forward, and after she had, five others did too.

"Anyway, the case was coming up, but even if he'd been found guilty, he wouldn't have been in jail long. His wife was planning to testify on his behalf. So was half the school board. He ruined that girl's life, Sian. She couldn't cope, she turned to drugs, and she ended up dead one night from an overdose."

Sian remembered. It was one of the few times she'd paid attention to the news. She'd thought at the time how fortunate she was to have the entire Ellis family behind her, protecting her, always.

"Nick killed the teacher before it went to court, and a whole lot of people felt a whole lot better whether they wanted to admit it or not."

Sian couldn't process it all. She heard what he was saying. She understood the logic of it but still... It seemed to her that by setting themselves apart, by deciding they had the right to mete out punishment, the Ellises had forgotten they were human.

"We made this area great!" Gavin said emphatically. "It is what it is because of us. People are safer because of us. Corruption is less because of us. We've made a difference. A good difference."

She didn't respond. It's not that she thought he was wrong. He wasn't. Not really. But she also couldn't agree. It was too hard to agree. She couldn't get the imagined screams of those poor children Agnes had terrorized out of her head.

"Why are you here?" Gavin asked abruptly.

"What do you mean?"

"Why didn't you just head west to California and never look back?"

"Because you're my family. All of you."

"So you're saying it's alright to kill for family but not for community?"

"What?" She felt like she was back in that pretend courtroom being cleverly outplayed by the defense.

"If it was just some random Goldenite up there, not Louise, would you say 'let the police handle it'?"

Sian didn't want to answer, because the fact of the matter was she would. If it wasn't Louise she wouldn't think twice about it. She wouldn't have put her life in danger to protect just anyone. She wouldn't have killed to protect just anyone.

Shame filled her. They were better than her. The Ellises were insane, they didn't understand moral lines or laws, they made decisions that weren't theirs to make, but they did it in the name of community, in the name of protection, in the name of a higher good. Just like Jack had taught them.

They put their lives on the line; they sacrificed any type of personal wants; they lived, breathed, and died Jack's mission: to remove corruption wherever it was found.

"It's the nowhere time," she murmured as Gavin turned up their driveway.

"The perfect time," they both said together.

"Jinx," she said. He laughed, and she punched him lightly in the arm. "Laughing counts. Ellis rules."

"I thought you didn't like the rules," Gavin said.

"I don't like SOME of the rules."

"Can we at least agree that we need to kill King and save Louise?"

"Yep."

"Then let's do it," he said. "And we'll argue about everything else later."

Eddie hadn't said anything for a while, but now he said, "They're still there."

"Good," Gavin said. "You stay in the car. If King manages to get away, follow him and call Nick for backup."

"Nick was on the list," Sian said softly.

"You don't know Nick the way I do."

That was true. She didn't know any of them the way he did. "Did Frank really start it?"

"Yes."

"Why did you kill Susan?"

"I killed three Ellises today," Gavin said, parking the car behind the converted carriage house garage. "But I did it to protect the rest."

"Explain it to me," she said.

"Right now?"

"Yes, right now."

He shook his head, and she knew he was thinking she was being stubborn, but she had to know.

"I killed Frank because he challenged my right to rule. There are a set of rules, Sian. Every single Ellis knows the rules, and they swear to abide by them. One of the rules is you cannot challenge the head of the Elliscs."

"Why not?"

He sighed heavily, then said, "Because I was trained from birth to lead our family. I understand the whys of our family. I understand the rules. I understand the criteria, the evaluation process. If everyone is vying for leadership the whole thing falls apart."

"So is that why you killed Susan?"

"I killed Susan because she was conspiring with Alistair, and Alistair tried to kill you. I don't know what their plan was, but it was a danger to all the Ellises. Furthermore, killing them set an example to all the Ellises that I am not to be messed with."

He sounded so much like their dad when he explained it all. It could have been a passage from his journal, explaining why he'd killed Sian.

She studied him, seeing the weight of it on his shoulders. He'd honestly killed them to protect everyone else, but it weighed heavily on him. It hurt him. It caused him pain.

I'm not wrong, she thought sadly. They might have good intentions. They might even have done a lot of good. But it was too much power, too much control and dominance. She simple couldn't imagine Gavin doing this for another fifty years. If only he would walk away. If only he would let Jack's legacy die.

Chapter Twenty

Volume 3; Entry 73; **Jack Ellis***:*

It amuses me that my home is in every way a manor of old. I built in secret passageways, making sure each crew of men was shifted enough that none of them knew the extent of the house. The only man who knows is my architect, and he will soon be gone.

I chose him to design my house not only because he is a master of his work but also because he owns majority control in one of the largest whore houses in the area.

Once he's finished with the final touches, I will eliminate him and his partners and shut the whore house down. Bronwen has built her own enterprise, which she will invite the women to work at. She is quite the crusader, my Bronwen.

"We'll sneak up through the cellar," Gavin whispered as they slowly circled the house.

"Through the cellar?"

"Right, I forgot."

"Forgot what?"

"The house is full of hidden passageways."

"No way!" Sian gasped.

"Yes way."

Sian pushed away a whisper of irritation and resentment. She'd deal with all that later once Louise was safe. "So how do we get there?" she asked.

"Through the cellar," Gavin said, rolling his eyes.

"I don't know where the cellar is," Sian ground out. "We never used it."

"Right, sorry. It's off the kitchen."

Alder's SUV had been parked by the front door. He had to know they would be able to track Louise's phone. He had to know they would come after him. She didn't understand what his game was. It seemed as if he should be running back to England as fast as possible.

"So what's our plan?" she whispered as they crept around the side.

"Do you remember when we were kids, and we used to play save the hostage? It's just like that."

It annoyed her that it kept coming back to that. Just like a game of this or that. How had she never noticed what they were really doing?

"We're not kids anymore," she hissed. "This isn't a game!"

"It never was," Gavin replied as he pulled back a section of sod to reveal a metal door.

Sian sighed heavily. It had always been a game to her. She'd never realized their entire life had been training. Training to be murderous assassins.

She could see it now. Now that all the little pieces were laid out. Their study of anatomy and criminology, jiu jitsu and fencing, every game they'd ever played, every trip, every book they'd read had been designed to turn them into perfect killers.

Gavin pulled open the hatch door and turned to face her. "Look Sian, you were right there with us. You have all the same training I do. Do you think you'd have made it this far if you didn't?"

He was right. She wouldn't have. The Ellises may not have wanted her, but they had certainly prepared her. She smiled just a little, feeling sick to her stomach.

"Okay," she said. "Let's save the hostage."

He winked at her, then disappeared into the darkness of the cellar. Sian followed him, and after a second a flashlight flared to life, lighting the space around them.

"Passage is over here," Gavin whispered as he led the way.

Sian couldn't help noticing how clean it was and how few cobwebs there were. The Ellises were prepared, always. They hadn't invited a war, but they had certainly been ready for one.

He pulled open a hidden door, and they started climbing. Every now and then he would pause and listen, but neither of them heard anything, so they continued slowly upwards.

"There's a passage that runs into the master suite," Gavin whispered.

Sian grabbed his hand. "What do you mean?"

"What do you mean 'what do I mean'?"

"There's a passage up to the master suite?"

"Yes."

"Then why did they die?"

"What?"

"Alice, Grandma, and Dad. Why didn't they just run out?"

Gavin stared at her for a second before shrugging and saying, "I don't know."

"They were already in the secret room; they had plenty of time to get out and circle around or whatever."

"Maybe they didn't have time," Gavin said. "Maybe they were right behind them. I don't know, but right now we need to find Louise."

Sian didn't argue, just followed him down the narrow hidden passageway. After a while, Gavin paused and whispered, "The hidden room is just on the other side."

Something crashed against the wall, and Sian jumped, smothering her gasp with her hand.

"WHERE IS IT?!!!" Alder shouted on the other side.

"I don't know what you're looking for!" Louise snapped. "I didn't even know this room was here! Just let me go! It's Gavin you want."

Sian swallowed a growl and reminded herself that Louise was just trying to buy time. As pretend hostages they'd all promised whatever they'd needed to promise in order to get free. There was no honor among people, only among Ellises.

"No!" Alder ground out. "I need all of you. All of you dead! And I need the ring!"

Ring? "What ring?" Sian whispered in Gavin's ear. He shook his head, and they continued to listen.

"Just call Gavin," Louise declared. "Call him, tell him you have me, get him to come here, and ask him where the ring is. He's the only one who will know."

"Do you think I'm a fool?!" Alder snapped. "I'll deal with Gavin when I have an army behind me."

"You're scared!" Louise laughed. "Of Gavin! He's nothing. He's a fraction of the man his father was. He doesn't have the stones to lead the Ellises, and you're scared of him."

"Do you think I'm a fool?" Alder snarled. "He's killed more of my men on his own than the rest of you put together."

"He's walking the other way," Gavin murmured. "On the count of three we bust through the door. I take King; you get Louise out."

Sian nodded. She was scared to death. What if Alder shot them both? What if Louise was already hurt? What if Gavin lost?

"One, two, three."

Gavin suddenly pushed the door in and jumped through, tackling Alder and taking him to the floor. The entire room shuddered from the impact, and Sian watched spellbound as Alder rolled to the side, but before he could escape, Gavin caught his foot and pulled him back down.

"Sian!" Louise snapped from the doorway. She was kneeling on the floor, hands zip tied in front of her, then zip tied to an exposed and blackened wall stud.

"Louise! Are you okay?" Sian gasped, running towards her.

"I'm fine," Louise said with a crooked smile. "Took you long enough!"

Sian laughed, glad to see Louise still had her sense of humor. She quickly cut the zip ties and turned to check on Gavin. He and Alder were rolling across the floor, kicking up ash and dust, but Gavin had that determined look on his face. The one that told Sian he was about to win.

Gavin swung his leg over King's chest and shoved his elbow into King's neck, holding him to the floor. It was time to finish it. With his free hand he ripped his knife from it sheath and buried it deep into King's chest.

King's eyes widened, he bucked one more time, then he gasped and fell still. Gavin ripped his knife out and shoved it back in a few times, just for good measure. He wasn't taking any chances.

In fact... He stood, gripping King's hair, and put his knife to the base of King's throat, cutting through the flesh and slicing through the muscles and tendons. When he hit the bone, he jerked King's head out straight and cut right through the vertebras.

"There!" he gasped in satisfaction. King was dead. Gavin had paid his debt. He'd exacted revenge. The balance was restored.

He turned toward the door, wondering if Sian had gotten Louise safely out.

"No," he breathed, feeling like the floor had just been cut out from under him. "Not you."

"Yes me, damn it! Why the hell can't you just die? You have more lives than a cat, but I've got you now!"

Tears streamed down Sian's face, but she stood perfectly still because Louise's knife tip was pushing into her back, just above her hip. All Louise had to do was give her knife a little shove and Sian was dead.

"I'm sorry, Gavin," Sian mouthed.

"She was on your list," he said sadly. "I just didn't believe it."

"List?" Louise demanded. "What list?"

"Sian made a list of all the Ellises who might carry a grudge."

"And you put me on it?" Louise asked, voice heavy with disbelief.

"You were so in love with Noah, you were heartbroken when Dad said no," Sian said softly. Sian's hand moved ever so slightly, and Gavin shook his head. "Why?" Sian asked. "Why?"

"Why?! I've given up everything for this family! Any semblance of a normal life! I would've sacrificed my children on the altar of Ellis! And I only ever asked for one thing. ONE! Noah!"

For once Gavin didn't know what to do. He was still holding both his knife and King's head, but he couldn't risk startling Louise. If she flinched even a little she would kill Sian.

His only hope was to keep her talking long enough that Eddie got curious and came in from behind her. "How?" Gavin asked. "How did you know about King?"

She laughed, eyes glazed with madness. "I didn't, but I was so angry at Uncle Edward that I thought I'd find a way to get even with him. I started watching him, and I discovered this room and started sneaking in. I read all the journals. God, we're a sick family! We deserve to die, you know?"

Every move she made, every time she gestured with her hand, the knife moved into Sian's side. Gavin could see just a bit of red on its tip, and he knew she was drawing blood.

Sian just stared at him with huge, terrified eyes. He had to save her. If he failed in this, he failed in everything. He needed her to live.

"So you found the journals?" he said, sliding his feet half an inch closer.

"Yes, and I learned all about Jack and his real family. The Winterset's."

"The Winterset's, really?" Gavin shuddered. "I can see why Jack changed his name." Sian's lips tweaked up, and Gavin winked at her. Louise was out of her mind, but if they played this right, they could still walk away. They WOULD still walk away.

"I sent them several newspaper articles. The Ellis family's greatest hits, if you like," Louise said, laughing just a bit. "I made sure to include all of Grandpa Jack's appearances. Only an idiot wouldn't have been able to figure it out, and the Winterset's aren't idiots."

"I still don't get why they care," Gavin said.

Louise laughed. "I can't believe you still don't get it! Jack was the Winterset heir! As long as even one of his heirs exists, the heir could claim the Winterset title, fortune, and lands."

Gavin stared at her for a moment, trying to determine if she was serious. He honestly hadn't paid that much attention when their tutor had explained the English class system, and he found it hard to believe that someone could just show up and claim to be the heir and everyone would believe them.

"I think I'm starting to get it," he drawled, hoping Eddie was coming already. "But surely not without some kind of proof."

"Oh, you mean like the Winterset family crest ring I found in the hidden passageway?"

Gavin blinked. He honestly hadn't seen that coming. Now he understood what Alder was looking for.

"Yeah, like that, I guess," he muttered.

He couldn't believe this was Louise. His Louise. They were cousins. They were friends. They'd had so many adventures together, so many moments.

He remembered holding her hand as they'd crossed over a raging river one day. He had been nine years old and she was only six. She'd been so confident in him, so assured that as long as she held his hand she'd be okay. He couldn't believe she had betrayed them, that she wanted them dead, that she wanted HIM dead.

"Do you realize what you've done?!" he demanded, suddenly furious. "How could you?!"

"Nothing!" she screamed, face purple with rage. "I've done nothing! Uncle Edward is dead, but you're still alive, and I can't be free until the head of the Ellises is dead! YOU!!!"

"You killed Uncle Danny," Sian whispered.

Louise faltered for a moment. "I didn't think... I mean... He wasn't the heir..." Her eyes hardened; and she snarled, "It will be worth it."

Her hand suddenly moved, and the knife was pointed at Gavin. He tossed King's head at her face, hoping she'd let go of Sian, and brought up his own knife so he could throw it as soon as she gave him an opening.

As soon as Louise moved her knife, Sian grabbed Louise's wrist with one hand forcing her knife down and used her other hand to rip out one of her hair pins. Louise hissed angrily, fighting against her and trying to turn the knife on Sian.

Alder's head suddenly slammed into Louise's face, and she and Sian stumbled into the wall together. Louise tore free from Sian's grip and leaped towards Gavin with a fierce cry.

"NO!!!" Sian screamed, jumping forward and seizing Louise's hair, ripping her backwards. "I'm sorry," Sian whispered, then slammed her hair pin into Louise's ear with all her might.

Louise's eyes turned dark with confusion. "Damn you," she whispered, eyes beginning to glaze. Then Gavin's knife tore through her throat, jerking her body from Sian's grasp. Sian watched Louise fall to the floor and stared at her lifeless body, tears pouring down her cheeks.

"I can't believe it was her," she whispered.

"You put her on the list," Gavin said, wrapping his arm around Sian's shoulders.

"I didn't really believe it. I was just trying to be thorough." Sian mumbled. She'd only asked her to be sure, and when Louise had denied it, she'd honestly believed her.

Sian had felt so hurt and betrayed when she'd learned her family was lying to her and excluding her from their lives. But knowing it was Louise who had set Alder on them, that Louise was responsible for Owen and Alice's deaths, that Louise wanted Gavin dead, made Sian furious. And sick. And sad. And she'd killed her. She'd killed her favorite cousin.

"You can't really blame her," Gavin murmured.

"I can!"

"You can't. She's right. We're monsters. We were born to demons, and we are demons."

"That's not true!" Sian snapped. "There's a lot of good you do. You said so yourself."

"Yeah, I don't know," Gavin sighed. "I mean, look at this mess. King was willing to kill all of us to protect the Winterset legacy, and I was willing to kill all of them to protect the Ellis legacy. It's really kind of ridiculous, don't you think?"

"That's not true!" Sian snapped.

"How's it not true?"

"You were willing to kill all of them to protect the Ellises. It's totally different. You don't care about money or possessions or power or status."

Gavin's forehead creased, and he said, "So?"

"So, you numbskull, if Alder had come and said he could legally take away every single penny the Ellises had, all their homes, their status, their place in society, would you have killed him?"

"Maybe," Gavin replied. "Alder seemed a bit corrupt if you ask me. He took locals hostage, and I think he would use anything and everything at his disposal to get what he wanted. So yeah, maybe I would've killed him, because otherwise he would have used our wealth and status for evil."

Sian smiled at him. "You'll make an excellent head of the Ellis family."

"I'm not sure I want to," Gavin said, eyes guarded.

"What are you saying?"

"I'm saying I think it's time for a change. I'm saying I think it's time Jack's legacy was laid to rest. I'm saying I think I don't want to be an Ellis anymore."

"Seriously?"

"Seriously."

Sian stared at him for moment, remembering all the times they'd celebrated being Ellises. She couldn't believe he'd even dream of just letting it go, of letting everything go.

But he was right. The family was too big, too different, even if he could keep it together for now it would eventually fall. It was the perfect time to end it.

"Fine," she agreed. "But I hate the name Suzy Roberts. I'm not going by Suzy."

Gavin burst out laughing. "I don't know," he chuckled. "I think you pass for a Suzy."

"No, not happening. No doing. Find me a new name."

"Alright," Gavin said, smiling at her. "But you're not Suzy yet. We still have a lot of work to do.

Chapter Twenty-One

Volume 66; Entry 110; **Jack Ellis***:*

Henry, my son, my heir, writes this final entry for me. I can see Bronwen across the room, waiting for me, and she looks just as she did the day I first saw her. Her smile is so bright, and I feel she must have forgiven me. It makes my heart soar with lightness.

I have built a legacy of which I am proud. I see every day the results of my efforts, the goodness I have created, and it makes me glad. I am pleased to know it will continue, in perpetuity, from one generation to the next to the next and the next.

I am pleased to pass away knowing I left the world a brighter place than when I entered it, that I left hope and promise behind me.

Bronwen beckons me. I must go. How I have missed you, my love.

Sian stared at Louise while Gavin searched the room and Alder's pockets. She just couldn't believe it had been Louise all along. If she hadn't been here, if she didn't have the cut in her back from Louise's knife to prove it, she still wouldn't believe it.

Louise had betrayed them. Louise had killed Alice, Owen, Mom, Grandma and Dad, and Uncle Danny. She had killed Joseph and his wife and children. She had killed all the Ellises that had died in the firefight. She had killed them all. She was the monster.

If she wanted to be free so badly she should have just run away and hidden, carved out a new life far from the Ellises just like Jack had done. She could have had Noah. All she had to do was leave. Why hadn't she? Why had she stayed?

Her plan hadn't been logical, Sian thought as she knelt down and slid Louise's eyelids closed. Her plan was petty and emotional and stupid. It hadn't been the well thought out plan of an Ellis. Not at all. Louise should have left. She should have never tried to kill them all.

Sian stared at the hair pin sticking out of Louise's ear. She had killed her. She had killed her favorite cousin. She had killed Louise. To protect Gavin. To protect all the Ellises. All this time she had been angry at her father for being willing to kill her. She'd been angry at him for even thinking about killing her. And here she had killed Louise.

It would have been funny if it wasn't so damn sad. "I'm sorry," she whispered, wanting to pull the hair pin from Louise's ear, wanting to cover her with a blanket or move her where no one would see her. She loved Louise. She truly loved her. Seeing her dead made her want to scream and wail. She hated that she'd had to kill her. But she hadn't had a choice. She'd had to kill Louise to protect everyone else.

"Found the ring," Gavin said, unhooking a chain and pulling it from around Louise's neck.

"She was carrying it with her?"

"Looks like. Matches the one on King's hand, but older and stuff." He stared at it for a moment, then held it out to her. "Does it look familiar to you?"

She took the ring, still warm from Louise's skin and looked at it. "Vaguely," she said after a moment.

"Jack altered the crest slightly," Gavin said, "But it's exactly like the emblem he stamped on all his buildings."

Gavin was right. It was the emblem stamped on every single Ellis building. Jack may have left his heritage behind, but he had managed to keep just a little bit of it.

She stared at the ring for a moment, feeling a strange sense of weight from it. In another life, as a different man, Jack Ellis had worn this ring and carried out a very different type of murder. She rolled the ring over, wondering if he'd felt relieved to be free of it.

"Oh hell!" she gasped. "Do you realize what this means?"

"No?"

"It means YOU'RE the Winterset heir!"

Gavin stared at her, eyes wide with shock, then they both burst out laughing.

"Can you imagine it?" he laughed. "Me, drinking tea and walking around all serious like! Maybe with a cane!"

"You could have tea with the queen!" she exclaimed. "And you could talk about the weather or, I don't know what they actually talk about, maybe polo?"

He shook his head, eyes bright with mirth. "Sounds fascinating, but I think I'll pass."

She giggled once more, then remembered where they were and that Louise was lying dead at her feet. She slipped the ring into her pocket and asked, "Were you serious earlier?"

His mirth faded, replaced with grief. "Yes. A hundred percent. I never wanted to be this person, this man. I wanted to go with you to Rome or California or Mexico. I wanted to pick up smoking hot ladies on the beach while you took photos of shells and sand."

Sian smiled at the thought. "So what're you going to do?"

"Disband the Ellises."

"You can do that?"

"Well, it's not in the rule book, but I'm the head of the Ellises. I can do what I want."

"Geez, Gavin, don't let it go to your head or anything."

He grinned. "For real. You have no idea the power I wield."

"I don't want to know."

"I mean, you want someone dead, anyone, bring it to me. If I agree with your request, it's done."

"Sounds great," Sian said, rolling her eyes.

"Remember that time you ordered double chocolate ice cream and the guy gave you vanilla?" Sian nodded. Gavin drew his finger across his throat. "Dead. We can't have corruption in the ice cream industry."

Sian giggled, but it wasn't really funny. He was serious in a way. He had that much power. The Ellises were the puppeteers behind the curtains, pulling everyone else's strings, and he was the puppeteer master.

"But what about the family?"

"Don't worry about the family. I'll take care of the family."

He was so confident, so relaxed, she had to believe him.

Gavin took one last look around the room and said, "I guess that's it. Let's go."

Sian gazed at the burned out room. The yellow tape that marked where her family's bodies had lain was still there. Louise was crumpled on the floor like a limp ragdoll. Alder's headless corpse was lying near the secret entrance, his blood mixing with the ash on the floor. This was Jack's legacy. Death.

Gavin stepped over Louise's body, then held his hand out to Sian. "It's almost over," he said.

She reached for him, relived that he was okay, that he was still whole, that he was still Gavin. Jack's legacy was dead. Their house was gone. Their family was gone. Life as they knew it was over and done, but as long as she had Gavin everything would be alright, just as it always had.

They walked down the hallway, side by side, and memories floated past her, filling her mind. Playing jail break in the house on rainy days. Slumber parties in her room with Louise. Tea in the garden with Grandma. Sitting at Grandpa's feet while he talked about the good old days. Racing Owen down the hallway to be the first to get a fresh cookie from the oven.

She could see it all so clearly. They were gone. They were gone, and she couldn't get them back. But they were still with her. They were always with her.

"I can hear Owen arguing with Alice," she said softly as they started down the stairs.

"What're they arguing about?" Gavin asked.

"I think he left his dirty socks in the hallway again."

Gavin chuckled. "Grandma will straighten them out."

"She always does." Sian smiled, imagining it all, then asked, "Do you think... if Dad had just let her marry Noah, do you think none of this would've happened?"

"I don't know."

They paused at the foot of the stairs and gazed at the yellow tape that had outlined their mother.

"You know how Grandpa would talk about the good old days?" Gavin asked. Sian smiled and nodded. "Remember how he used to say 'all things, especially good things, come to an end'? But then he said, 'the end of one thing is always the beginning of something else.'"

Sian could hear Grandpa saying it, deep voice drowning out the crackling of the library fire.

"I think it's like that," Gavin went on. "I think the Ellis family was a good thing, but it's come to an end. It's not a bad thing or a sad thing. It's just a new beginning. That's all."

They turned together, away from the kitchen, and the remains of Owen's last breakfast, and walked out the front door. Sian didn't look back. She couldn't look back at the house and see it the way it was, empty and sad. She had to remember it the way it used to be. Filled with laughter and love. Filled with her family.

They met Eddie ten feet from the door, gun drawn.

"Too late, Eddie," Gavin said. "It's all wrapped up."

"Where's Louise?"

"Dead."

Eddie's face paled. "Dead?"

"Dead. Let's go," Gavin said. "You drive, Eddie. Take us to Nick's."

*Volume 10; Entry 95; **Henry Ellis**:*

I actually considered it today. I looked at the map and I traced a line out to California. They say it's a land of plenty. I could go there and disappear. Henry Ellis no more.

But I cannot leave my family. I made my sons and daughters into this. I introduced their sons and daughters. I bear the weight of all this on my head, on my soul. It is my fault, my cross to bear.

If I could go back to that moment, the moment my father took me into town, the moment my father told me to kill that thieving, lying man of business, I would say 'no'. Just as I wanted to then.

I would open my mouth, I would say "no", and I would turn the knife on him, and kill him there so we could all be free. There is no hope for us now. We are caught in this bind, destined forever to be wicked.

"Alright," Gavin said, sitting down at Nick's kitchen table. "I need a piece of paper."

"What?" Nick asked.

"Paper, Nick. Paper and a pen! Now!"

"Alright. Don't get your boxers in a bunch," Nick grumbled, leaving the room and bringing back paper and a pen.

"Perfect, now leave me alone. Out; all of you!"

*Volume 1; Entry 1; **Gavin Ellis**:*

My father, Edward Ellis was murdered, along with several others members of the Ellis family. This all came about because one of our members was discontent with the Ellis rules.

Louise Ellis learned Jack's secrets and contacted someone whose greatest desire was to see Jack's entire bloodline wiped out. Although Alder King is now dead, the danger to the Ellises still exists.

As such, I am hereby disbanding the Ellis family. Each of you will start new lives, much as Jack originally did, and you will carve out a new place for yourselves in society, hopefully a much better place.

I know this will come as a shock to some of you and a relief to others. What I do now, I do ultimately to preserve Jack Ellis's true legacy: family.

We have stood together, side by side, and protected each other for almost a hundred and fifty years, and that is more important than any other tasks we may have completed.

But in addition to that, we have made a difference in our community. We have nothing to be ashamed of. We can hold our heads high. We are Ellises, and we have done what we have done.

Like our forefather Jack once did, it is time for each of us to forge a new beginning. We are strong, and even as Smith's or Jones's we can make a difference in the world around us.

However, since there will no longer be a structure to enforce the rules of the Ellis line, the checks and balances, I am forbidding each and every one of you from killing in the future. (Except if needed for self-defense.)

Never again will an Ellis decide the fate of another human being. I will be watching you, and if one of you crosses the line, I will remove you. I will do whatever it takes to protect our family, just as Jack, Henry, Richard, and Edward did before me.

I forbid you from telling anyone who doesn't already know, including your own sons and daughters. I forbid you from telling any future spouses. I forbid any of you who are already married from separating. You know the rules. I am not doing away with the rules. Each and every one of you has sworn to obey the rules, and I am holding you to it.

Gavin paused, uncertainty choking him. He had to decide. He couldn't be both. He was either one or the other. Gavin Ellis. Head of the Ellises. Defender of the Ellis family. Or nobody.

His hand tightened on the pen. He couldn't do it. He couldn't walk away. He was an Ellis. He would always be an Ellis.

I remain Gavin Ellis, head of the Ellis line, and if a day comes that we must all come together again, I know you will answer my call. But for today and tomorrow and the next day, I want you to live. I want you to be free.

Gavin reread his note several times. It didn't really say all he wanted it to say. It didn't say how much he would miss them or how much he enjoyed being with them and laughing with them. It didn't say how sad he was to let them all go, to end whatever this was.

It wasn't that he thought Jack was wrong. It wasn't that he thought the Ellises were wrong. They were only human, and they could certainly screw up, but he'd still say they'd changed things for the better.

The problem was twofold. Not only did he not want to be the one to guide everyone's lives, but he also honestly believed they were still in danger. Alder King had only been part of something. He wasn't the head. He was a hand. The only way the Ellises would be safe is if Gavin found the head and destroyed it.

"Sian, come here!" Gavin demanded.

"I'm not your damn lackey!" Sian snapped as she walked into the room.

"That's why I love you."

She rolled her eyes. "What do you want?"

"Read this."

"Please," she hissed.

Gavin grinned. "I'm glad you're still you."

"Me too."

"Please."

"Okay."

Sian sat at the table and read the note. He watched her facial expressions, wondering exactly what she was thinking. He watched her eyes move to the top as she read it again. Then she read it again. Finally she dropped the note and looked at him.

"Really?" she asked.

"Really."

"Just like that?"

"Yeah."

"Are you sure?"

"Yep."

"Okay."

Gavin glared at her. "Okay? That's it?"

"What do you want me to say? It sucks! I feel like you're killing our entire family. I mean we'll never see Nick again? Or David? Eddie? Aunt Jo? No one? Ever?" He shook his head. "Why?"

"As Ellises they all have a target on their backs. As nobodies... they'll be free."

"What will they do?"

"Start over. Nick wants to own a vineyard."

"Seriously?"

"Seriously. Can't you see Jilly jumping up and down in a grape vat?"

Sian laughed. "I can. I wonder what Louise would have done."

Gavin's face hardened. "Who knows. All I know is she stole the opportunity from other Ellises, like Owen and Alice and Joseph."

"I thought you said you couldn't blame her."

"I changed my mind."

Sian studied him for a moment before saying, "In a way she made it possible for Nick to have his vineyard."

"What do you mean?"

"If she hadn't contacted the Winterset's, Dad would have been the head for another thirty years or so. You know?"

Gavin closed his eyes, trying to imagine it. Edward Ellis growing old and dying of natural causes. Nick never left Golden. Owen married and had kids. Frank continued to secretly hate his wife. Uncle Danny kept fishing. Louise went slowly insane. And Gavin and Sian died.

"He would have eventually killed us both," Gavin said softly.

"I know," she whispered. "Anything to protect the Ellises. Why didn't you just leave and take me with you?"

"It's against the rules."

She laughed loudly. "I'm beginning to be glad Dad decided not to bring me in. It doesn't sound like much fun."

"Well, it's a lot of rules. And stuff. You know."

"I don't, but you'll tell me. Nick brought you the journals from Alder's."

Gavin flinched. "I wish he'd just burned them."

"Isn't there a rule about that?"

"Actually there is," he said with a chuckle.

"So what will you do?" Sian asked.

"Hunt down the Winterset's."

"Why?"

"They killed our family, Sian. I can't let that go. It's my job to protect the Ellises, to keep them safe, to watch over them. And as long as the Winterset's are roaming around, our family will never be safe."

Sian was quiet for a long time. She couldn't believe he was ending it. The Ellis family just done, gone, spread across the world. It felt so wrong, so final, so terrible.

She imagined him wandering London looking for Winterset's. How would he ever find them? Just Gavin all on his own? No Eddie to hack into stuff, no Nick to adjust the coroner's report, no Joseph or Uncle Fred to pull up information. It didn't seem possible. It was a fool's errand.

"Don't go," she said. "I'll be Suzy Roberts; you can be my brother Sam Roberts. We'll go to California and slum on the beaches. All the ladies will love you. Please!"

He shook his head. "You don't need me, Sian. You're strong, capable, and talented. You can go out into the world and succeed just like Nick and Eddie. Go be Suzy Roberts. Go live."

"I don't want to," she whispered. "Not without you."

"I can't leave the Ellises behind," he said, eyes serious and hard. "I can't. They're still my responsibility; they will always be my responsibility. I can't stop being Gavin Ellis. Not ever. I made a promise, and I intend to keep it. No matter what. But you're free. You don't have to be an Ellis anymore."

Fear rushed through her. He was going to leave her. He was going to leave her behind, and she would never see him again.

"Don't leave me," she whispered. "I don't care where you go, take me with you."

"I can't. I can't ask you to be an Ellis. I can't ask you to make those decisions."

"What do you mean?" It hurt too much, more than anything else so far. She couldn't imagine life without her brother at her side. Isn't that what they'd been fighting for this whole time?

"You said it yourself," Gavin said. "It's too much power, one man deciding who lives and dies. I'm that one man, Sian. I decide who lives and dies, and the Winterset's die."

Tears poured down her cheeks. She didn't understand why right now, in this moment, she was more terrified than she'd ever been in her life. It's not that she didn't think she could do it. It's not that she didn't think she could succeed in life. She knew she could.

She just didn't know what the point was if she was doing it without Gavin. She pretended to read his note again to give herself time to think. Could she follow him? Could she remain Sian Ellis? Not just in name but in everything the Ellis name stood for?

Alder King had killed her family. But he'd said himself he didn't care one way or the other. He'd done it because his father had ordered him to. Just like Edward had ordered Gavin to kill. The only difference being that Edward had ordered Gavin to kill someone he'd deemed corrupt. Alder's father had ordered Alder to kill an entire line because he was scared of the consequences if they lived.

Alder's father was corrupt by any definition, even changing ones. But more importantly, he'd started a war with the Ellises. And no one, absolutely no one, hurt the Ellises and got away with it.

Epilogue

*Volume 1; Entry 17; **Gavin Ellis**:*
Jack was right. London is beautiful. Although I wonder if he would still think so if he saw it today, with its strange array of modern buildings mixed in with old. I cannot wait to walk in his footsteps, to follow his path, to meet his family face to face.

Sian stepped off the bus onto a busy street. It didn't look anything like Jack had described. It was missing the black coal smoke and the hollering of vendors selling their wares. There weren't whores standing on every corner. There weren't children running wild down the streets, pickpocketing everyone they came across.

It all looked rather ordinary and modern. Colorful graffiti covered walls and hydrants, even some doors. People walked quickly past her, eyes trained on their cell phones. It wasn't all that different than home, and it was really kind of disappointing.

Sian had expected an aura or a vibration that just screamed "Jack was here!". But regardless of the billboards advertising tours of Jack's darkest hours, she couldn't see it. She couldn't begin to form a picture of the man who had brutally murdered defenseless women on these very London streets.

All she could see was the man who was her great-great-great grandfather. Jack Ellis had been a defender of the weak and helpless. He'd built homes for orphans. He'd employed hundreds of people. He'd fought for their rights both in the daylight and in the shadows.

It seemed so strange to her that he'd had his beginning here. It seemed wrong that he'd killed without thought. That he hadn't questioned 'why'. Not until Bronwen.

She paused on that fateful street corner. The one where Jack had almost killed Bronwen. If Bronwen hadn't smiled at him, everything would be different. Jack would have gone on killing whores at his father's direction, and the Ellises would have never been.

She glanced up at the tall buildings in the distance. London seemed so much vaster than Golden or Denver or Colorado. The Winterset's could be anywhere. They could be right in front of her, and she wouldn't know.

"I don't know about this, Gavin," she muttered as they crossed the street towards the Ten Bells Pub.

"It'll be alright, Sian," he replied, grabbing her hand and pulling her through the doorway. "It's just like a game of eliminate the dictator."

She followed him into the pub, grinning as the familiar smell of malt enveloped her. Gavin was right. They'd trained their entire lives for this.

Gerald Kingsley, Earl of Winterset, carefully set his glass of brandy on his desk. He leveled an even stare at his eldest son and said, "Tell me once more."

Ethan Kingsley cleared his throat and said, "Alder is dead. Everyone you sent with him is dead, and the Ellises have gone underground."

"Interesting. What of their leader?"

"Edward Ellis?"

"Yes."

"He's been confirmed deceased."

"And his son?"

"Gavin Ellis?"

"Yes."

"No. He is not deceased."

Gerald drank the remainder of his brandy in one swallow. He didn't know much about the Ellises, but he knew Alder. Of all his sons, Alder was the most brutal and efficient. Gerald had sent him to kill the Ellises with nearly one hundred and fifty men. This was not good.

"Call in the Elites," Gerald ordered. It was time to prepare for war.

Meanwhile, across the pond, in the house that Jack built, burned and ruined timbers were torn out and replaced with new.

The End

MY ONE AND ONLY

by M.M. **Boulder**

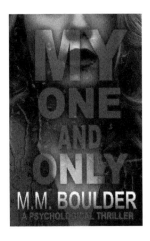

Nothing says "I love you" like dead bunnies and chocolates...

As much as Diana Flynn wants to run away, she can't. She's worked too hard to rebuild her life, and she's not going to let some sadistic stalker steal everything from her. Everywhere she goes, everywhere she turns, he's there. Following her, leaving her "presents" and notes, taking locks of her hair as she sleeps...

When the law can't help her, she's forced to take matters into her own hands and become the hunter instead of the prey.

To sign up to receive notice when this book releases please visit www.mmboulder.com

MY BETTER HALF

by M.M. **Boulder**

Till Death Do Us Part...

Lucille Stevenson has a secret.

Attacked at home by an unknown assailant, meek Lucille Stevenson **should be dead**, but she isn't. She should have called the police, she should have told her husband, she should have done a lot of things, but she didn't. Because what Lucille did to her attacker went far beyond self-defense.

It was cold, brutal, and vicious, and if anyone found out, **her life would be over**. Unfortunately, her secret isn't as safe as she thinks because **Lucille isn't the only one keeping secrets...**

Read now at Amazon.com

THE LAST DOOR

by M.M. **Boulder**

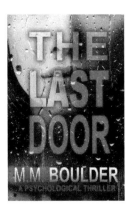

How far would you go to catch your mother's killer?

Amy Harrison knows something terrible happened to her parents; she just doesn't know what because she can't remember the first twelve years of her life. Determined to uncover the truth, Amy begins an experimental treatment to recover her lost memories, and **all she can see is blood.**

Blood. Whiskey. Pink. A voice. Someone who loved her. Someone she loved. **A killer. And death. So much death.** Convinced her chaotic flashes of memory are real, Amy keeps pushing forward **despite what it's doing to her**. But the further she goes, the more her memories take over her, pushing sweet Amy away and replacing her with someone else...

Will Amy be able to recover her past, learn the terrible secret that made her forget it all, and save her own life before she loses everything? Or is history doomed to repeat itself?

Read now at Amazon.com

THE LEGEND OF
ANDREW RUFUS

An Action/Adventure series for adults and teens alike
DARK AWAKENING (Book 1) Excerpt:

Andrew turned slowly, looking for something, anything, to shoot. There were dozens of distorted shapes surrounding him, but he couldn't see a black center in any of them. Suddenly the shapes began to move, and one tore into him so fast he barely saw it, but he felt it ripping across his leg. He jerked and pointed his gun towards it, but it was already gone. *Not yet!*

Pain shot through his shoulders as something tore across his back. Andrew bit his lip and held himself still. He could do this. He just had to wait for the right moment. He ignored a slash across his arms and fixed his eyes on one shape, watching it carefully. As it started moving towards him, Andrew kept his eyes on it, ignoring the other one that ripped across his face, ignoring the pain in his legs and back.

The dust devil came closer and closer, and suddenly Andrew saw it. Just a tiny bit of black in the center of a grey mass of dirt and thorns. He aimed and fired, and dust spewed everywhere, coating Andrew in debris. He fixed his eyes on another one. They were attacking so fast now Andrew felt like he was a speed bag. He could barely catch his breath before another hit him, and every time one tore across him, his body cried out in hot pain. He swiped blood out of his eyes and fired again. A dust devil exploded.

He fired again and again, reloading and reloading, until he ran out of ammo, and then he pulled one of his knives. His whole body stung. Blood was oozing into his palm, but he just gripped the knife tighter. He only had two knives, so he knew he couldn't throw them. He'd never be able to find them again, and then he'd be weaponless. The absolute pure fear and dread that clawed at him sharpened everything, making everything clearer. He wasn't going to die like this. Not in Pecos's body. Not here. Not now.

Read now at Amazon.com

Printed in Great Britain
by Amazon